JOURNEY GIRLS

Penny Davis

Published by Mindstir Media, LLC

45 Lafayette Rd | Suite 181| North Hampton, NH 03862 | USA

1.800.767.0531 | www.mindstirmedia.com

Printed in the United States of America

ISBN-13: 978-1-7354785-3-1

MINDSTIR MEDIA

PROLOGUE

An unforgettable story about the power of women and their life-long friendships. Helping and healing, these women watch a mystery unfold in modern-day Savannah.

Meghan Kingston, an Interior Decorator opened Marigold's an interior design business complete with a classroom and complimented with an antique shop and garden. Ellie Hall inherited Annabelle's Bakery from her grandmother and expanded the business to include a trendy breakfast cafe. Meg and Ellie have been best friends since they wore their Brownie uniforms to troop meetings in second grade.

Anna, Ellie's daughter is an amazing spirited young girl wise beyond her nineteen years. She is an art student at SCAD which perfectly matches her vibrant personality.

Jenny Thompson is attending a writers' conference in Atlanta when she decides on a whim to drive the three hours to Savannah, to buy her mother, Karen Ashland, a birthday gift from her mother's childhood hometown. She intends to buy a beautiful vintage cake stand to display her mother's 70th birthday cake. But, Jenny discovers much more than a birthday gift in Savannah; she also discovers a story that forges friendships and careers out of tragedy.

Miss Kate, well, she is a delightful surprise to everyone.

And, then there is "Lovey," the little girl ghost who wears a pink sundress, pigtails and the half heart gold necklace. She appears so often in Meg's mirrors that Meg isn't sure if she still lives there or just loves to visit.

Dedication

To best, old, new, writing, cafe, antique, gardening and career friends .....and to those I hope to meet soon. My mother always said, "To have a friend you have to be a friend."

Other books by Penny Davis

"PJ's, Pearls, and Fishing Poles"

A loving story about Hospice honoring patients,
families and caregivers.

Table of Contents

Part One

A VINTAGE SOUL

CHAPTER 1

Introduction

I was startled awake, my heart pounding in my chest to the rhythm of the pounding on my front door that changed my life ten years ago. But this time it was just a dream. Or it would be, except that it still seemed very real. The ceiling fan whirled above my head, creating a light breeze as I lay quietly, trying to steady both my heartbeat and a head full of memories.

"Oh Jack," I sighed out loud, to no one. "I miss you so much." After a few minutes, I closed my eyes and pulled the lightweight summer quilt up to my shoulders. Because the hour was so early, I tried to drift off to sleep again, but I knew it would never happen. Instead, I watched the clock hands move ever so slowly.

Two hours later, it was only seven o'clock, but at least the sun was beginning to peek through the white wooden slats of my bedroom shutters on this mid-March day. I stretched out in bed, looking around the room. My recently painted pale pink walls were in sharp contrast to the crisp white of the shutters and the trim surrounding the windows. The vintage walnut sleigh bed was a wedding gift that Jack and I had bought each other fifteen years ago. The soft quilt, a wedding ring pattern, had probably been crafted more than a hundred years before our wedding. It was impossible to know its age exactly, but to me it was priceless, both for the symbol of a happy wedding and the memories it inspired of my early married days. A rare find when I was just starting my collections and my plans for an interior design shop to be named Marigold's. Even though by then I had been made a recent widow, the thought of the wedding ring pattern still gave me comfort.

Despite the passing of a decade since Jack's death, sometimes, like this early morning, the enormity of what happened seemed incomprehensible. It could have occurred ten years ago or ten minutes ago, the pain still seemed so immediate. I sat up in bed to gaze at a room full of memories. I could almost hear Jack whispering sleepily, *"Love you, love of my life."*

When I finally managed to crawl out of bed and cross the old hardwood floor in my bare feet, I glanced, as I always do, at the antique cherry oval mirror above the chest. I smiled at the little girl who smiled back at me from within the mirror. She was wearing a pink sundress, pigtails, and half of a gold heart dangling on a necklace. I saw her so frequently that I wasn't sure if she truly lived here in my house or just loved to visit. I named her "Lovey" because someone must be missing her, someone must love her.

"Good morning, Lovey," I said, just as I always did.

She nodded, with an endearing expression on her face.

Somehow this little girl ghost had become a comfort to me. She appeared in mirrors all over the house and shop. Often I thought that I could hear a giggle, but at other times I suspected I could catch faint crying sounds. I totally understood both emotions.

I puttered around the room, smoothing the linens, fluffing pillows, and making the bed. The cherry dresser's patina was as smooth as silk, so it reflected the antique silver frames resting on its surface. Photos of Jack and me. Our wedding day fifteen years earlier. Jack's graduation from law school three days before our wedding. Me, holding my diploma on my graduation day, when I earned my degree in interior design. Me, hanging out a shingle in front of my first business that same summer. And, the two of us standing proudly in front of our first home. This home.

We were full of plans in those days, I reminded myself, staring at that photograph. But all of those plans on our shared to-do list had come to a screeching halt ten years ago. That's when the pictures stopped, too.

I lingered a moment longer, staring at the photographic progression of our lives together before I crossed the room towards the bathroom, talking to myself—just one of my bad habits. I mumbled to myself and Lovey, "I'm so glad that I decided not to move after it happened."

The floorboards creaked, and once again I thought of the history of this house. Jack and I had often speculated about the unknown people who had called this place home throughout the century before we appeared on the doorstep. We had signed the deed and moved in soon after we married. Fifteen years ago seemed a very long time to me on this particular morning.

As soon as our signatures dried on the deed, Jack and I had immediately begun creating our to-do list of home projects, which was as long and big as our dreams had been. But, we only had five years to dream and work together. Jack's quick trip to the hardware store on our fifth anniversary crossed with the path a drunk driver was taking. It was the fatal car crash and a policeman's knock on my front door that afternoon that changed everything. Forever.

My memories were jerked back to reality when I heard a noise, a key turning in the back door. "Hi, Ellie," I called out, anticipating the visitor was my closest and dearest friend. "Is that you? This early?"

The reply wasn't from Ellie, however. "Hey, Meg, it's me, Anna. Mom sent me over to bring you fresh granola for your apothecary jar and a peach scone for breakfast. I'm feeding Lucy for you as long as I'm here, and I'll stop by the shop to drop off some of Mom's treats, so gotta run. I'm on my way to class. Love you!" All of that in one breath. I didn't even have time to squeeze in a "Thank you!" before I heard the side door slam shut.

"Love you, too, sweet girl," I said to the quiet room.

Anna was Ellie's precious daughter. Ellie had been my best friend since we both wore Brownie uniforms to troop meetings in the second grade. She and

Anna were a big part of the reason why I decided to stay in this big old house, and I am very grateful. My home is now part of my heart, my soul, and my history. And, if it wasn't for Anna, I'd probably still refuse to answer any knocks that sounded on the front door.

Anna was nine when Jack died, and she seemed to have an intuitive sense of the pain I was going through. She didn't miss a thing, she understood that I just couldn't answer the front door for fear of the vision of that policeman who had come to deliver the dreadful news. Over the coming months, family members and friends got used to my requests to use the side door to enter into my kitchen.

A year later, with all of the wisdom of an ten-year-old, Anna solved my problem one day. I was painting the kitchen a beautiful pale yellow, trying to resume projects on the to-do list still hanging on the refrigerator, when I heard noises on the front porch. I went to investigate and found Anna hanging a cardboard sign on the front door—on the nail previously used for the funeral wreath, a custom belonging to the heritage of the Old South. The little sign was painted and then covered in glitter. A childish script announced, "'WELCOME" and it dangled from a thick piece of yarn.

"Honey, what are you doing?" I had asked her.

"I'm helping, of course." Anna replied. "You have to stop using just the side door and start using your front door again. This sign will tell people to come visit." And then, as if to seal the deal, she added, "My Jack said it was okay." I was speechless. The sign has continued to hang there all these years later, tattered and faded, but no less meaningful. I can't take it down. And I learned that she, too, still cherished the close bond she had shared with Jack.

Watching Anna enter Marigold's, my thoughts quickly shifted to my shop. Marigold's stands just beyond my back garden. Like everything in my world, the shop has been a work in progress in the years since Jack left us. I love the people I meet there every day. Some come searching for design tips or a discussion about garden designs; others come searching for an antique chest, a piece of white ironstone, or to replace an item they broke or remember from their grandmother's house.

Shortly after Jack died, I decided that this adorable old stone cottage, which had once served as a caretaker's home for our property, would be the perfect place for my business. With a lot of help from my friends, we turned it into a charming office/antique shop/classroom, where I could work with clients seeking renovations or design changes for their homes.

I have always loved blending the new and the old, developing my own unique style. Little by little, I added classes to my schedule and then a few vintage items, which were originally intended to give clients visual decorating ideas. Now the shop is full, top to bottom, with vintage furniture, glassware, quilts, baskets, Depression glass, linens, quilts, and my passion for white ironstone pottery. I make appointments to visit clients in their homes to plan remodeling, but I love doing business in my cottage shop too.

The yard has changed, too. What was once an open green space between my home and shop gradually became a huge garden. It started with a few rose bushes, but quickly became a luxurious and picturesque beds of vegetables, flowers, flowering trees, bushes, and herbs. Along the way, I added Adirondack chairs for relaxing and an umbrella table with eight chairs for outside dining. Almost without knowing it, my backyard garden became a beautiful, fragrant, peaceful haven—for my clients as well as for me—as I continued to develop my business.

The garden is full of the blooms that make Savannah so picturesque: everything from jasmine to sunflowers and roses. Honeysuckle climbs a tall trellis. Fluttery butterfly bushes, lilac bushes, and borders of boxwood lure birds and butterflies. Lemon balm, I learned as I began studying horticulture, lessens anxiety, so I planted mounds of it. Lavender clumps wind around bird feeders and stone benches; its pungent fragrance offers a welcome essence of tranquility.

I smiled as I saw Anna swiftly lock Marigold's door and dash in the direction of her car. After a quick shower, I dressed in a pair of blue capris and a white linen shirt with the sleeves rolled up before slipping my feet into a pair of black leather strappy sandals. I was ready to embrace warm weather. Clasping my gold cuff bracelet engraved with *Jack* around my wrist, I twisted my wide gold wedding band for good luck, smiling as I remembered the day Jack slipped it onto my ring finger.

Since I turned forty on my previous birthday, I sometimes found myself glancing in the mirror and studying my short sassy cut, looking for a stray gray hair among the mass of brown. Happily for me, I didn't find any today. However, I did see a pair of soulful but happy chocolate-brown eyes gazing back at me. They seemed to say, *"Everything is all good, so go start your day."* That was a choice I had made years earlier, when I decided I would refuse to become a victim. Despite the intense pain I suffered, I managed to survive—and, with the help of friends, even begin to thrive.

I puttered around the kitchen, pouring a cup of coffee to enjoy with my peach scone, then sat on a stool beside my new-to-me kitchen island, formally an old hardware counter. I had topped both the island and my counters with maple butcher block after I white-washed the cabinets. When I installed the island, I changed all the door knobs and handles, using some great vintage hardware I'd found at a dusty old antique shop going out of business. No trendy granite countertops for me! I love the look and feel of chopping on a butcher block. The country atmosphere, highlighted by a row of tomatoes ripening on my windowsill, gave me such peace.

The room was still a work in progress, but I liked it that way. The pale yellow walls are complemented by a painting of bright yellow sunflowers Anna had painted and given me a couple of birthdays ago. The original hardwood floors gleamed in the early morning sun as I moved over to my breakfast nook with my coffee and the day's newspaper. I love sitting there, glancing past my little round table, to watch the birds at the feeders in my garden. That view starts my day every morning, giving me a sense of peace and beauty.

Beside my elbow sat a pile of decorating magazines I had promised myself to study when I found a quiet moment. Marigold's began as a dream outlined on a legal pad. Now it embodies the best of my degree in Interior Design and Master Gardener certificate, as well as my life-long passion for finding and placing interesting pieces of old furniture. My stash of antiques grew over the years, and my business expanded as I came to realize that any successful business focuses on the people, their stories, and the lives they hope to see unfold.

The early spring day was too lovely to stay indoors very long. I headed out to the garden and cut some fragrant pink roses for the cut-glass vase on my shop counter—the vase that sits next to my business cards and Ellie's cards for Annabelle's Bakery & Café. Her jar of free cookie samples was constantly emptied and constantly restocked every day, thanks to Ellie's generosity and Anna's deliveries. My goal was to have everyone leave Marigold's happy. An emotion that matters.

CHAPTER 2
Monday

I often schedule classes for Monday mornings—a great way to start a week productively and enjoyably. On this day, the class would focus on kitchen design. Eight ladies were registered. The long pine farm table would seat all of them, and we would be surrounded by the ambience of shop details and flowers. Ellie and I have an arrangement and she usually drops by to deliver a treat for class but today it was Anna delivering tangy lemon bars and chocolate brownies. The sweet treats would be served on vintage green Depression glass plates, and we would drink our sweet tea from an assortment of vintage glassware. This is, after all, a trademark of Southern hospitality.

I headed up the stone pathway to my shop with my coffee cup in my hand and my well-fed gray cat Lucy at my side. The window boxes were overflowing with flowers in early bloom on this beautiful day: recently planted red geraniums, white petunias, blue forget-me-nots, and asparagus fern. Lining the porch, big terra cotta pots rested on saucers, filled with luxuriant, brilliant orange and yellow marigolds. Green rocking chairs offered visitors a chance to catch their breath, consider a purchase, or sniff the fragrances from my garden. Friends often dropped by just to rock for several minutes—or hours—and enjoy the view of my gardens from those chairs.

I often marveled at the way many guests seemed to find their own sense of peace here, when they thought they were coming to find something in my shop. I flipped the orange painted sign—another Anna creation—from "closed" to "open," and started my day thinking about my goddaughter's vibrant, happy spirit. This particular sign displayed a little more sophistication in her artistry than the sign on the front door of my home.

The previous week I had purchased several boxes from an estate sale, and I was anxious to start sorting through them. I knew that I would find at least twenty pieces of beautiful blue-and-white sponge ware. Also assorted pieces of green Depression glass and white ironstone that several of my customers loved and collected. I always enjoyed their stories when they came regularly to browse. "I just have to have a platter like my grandma's for the Thanksgiving turkey." Or, "My mom always served soup in the family tureen on cold winter Sundays, and the tureen looked just like this."

As I opened a third box, I discovered old monogramed linens. After sorting through them, I laid the pile aside for laundering and pressing. Someone, I knew, would find a tea towel with the initial they wanted, either to keep or give as a gift. Just last week, a visitor who had eaten breakfast at Annabelle's found my Marigold's business card on her counter and followed Ellie's directions to my shop; she left with a car full of treasures to take home to the Midwest. As always, I snapped a picture of her and added it to my "Friendship Board." She was still talking about the beautiful needlework on a pair of pillowcases—"True works of art, something you can't find these days."—as her car pulled away from the curb and she returned my wave.

That same day, another customer came looking for vintage Fiestaware dishes—the originals, made in the 1930s, not the modern-day reproductions. She was only collecting the cobalt blue pieces as a gift for her daughter, she told me. We chatted as I showed her my stack of plates and bowls, and she commented that she wished she could leave her "Corporate America job" and all of its pressures and do something creative instead. "Something like you're doing," she said. She told me how tired she was of her career demands as her eyes swept around my shop.

"You seem so happy," she told me as we took seats beside my long pine table. She sounded so wistful.

I smiled at her. "Life is too short to live in a way that makes you unhappy. Make a wish for a new world and a new place for yourself in it," I suggested, adding, "Think about it. Make a plan." She began to cry. But, she nodded in agreement. I gave her a raisin cookie and a hug as she left Marigold's.

After she left, I smiled at Lovey, who smiled back at me from a tall silver framed mirror. I took a bottle of cold water to the garden and sat under the shade of the old oak tree, looking around the garden appreciatively. My garden hadn't always been this serene.

Something transformed it—and me—during the course of the last few years.

When Jack and I moved into our dream house fifteen years ago, we sat under this tree together as we spoke of ideas for our old house and I talked about plans for my first kitchen garden. "I'll plant an organic garden with tomatoes, peppers, cucumbers, scallions, lettuce, and a few herbs to add to our salads, pasta sauces, salsas, and omelets," I told him proudly, leaning on his shoulder and pointing to the future locations of my crops. I could barely cook in those days; over the years, both my gardening and my cooking have improved tremendously, just as Ellie's baking skills were improving and her business was beginning to flourish.

When we were little girls, Ellie and I used to stand on stepstools at Annabelle's Bakery, watching her grandmother mix, stir, roll, cut, and bake mouth-watering sweet treats and breads. Long ago, my friend and I decided that I would supply Ellie's family with salads and pasta sauces, and she would keep my kitchen and shop stocked with bakery items.

Before Marigold's existed anywhere but in my imagination, Jack and I had talked briefly about the possibilities for the little stone cottage, imagining what it had been like when it was newly built and imagining what it could become in the future. By that time, Jack had joined a law firm downtown and had a very nice and efficient office. I, on the other hand, still went to work every day in my small, cramped office space, which I leased in a vintage building that I loved but was too cramped for a growing business. But, I spent most of my time either in the car on my way to see a client or in their homes discussing plans, I reminded Jack.

"I'm constantly lugging catalogs, samples, swatches, and paint chips wherever I go," I told him. "What would you think if we converted the cottage to my office?" I asked Jack one lazy summer afternoon. "I could move my design business there, and maybe also start offering design and decorating classes."

"I think that's an excellent plan," Jack said, wrapping his arm around my shoulders. "Let's go for it." That very day we began discussing different ideas for renovating the dusty cottage, which had been filled with scraps of wood and discarded items by generations of people who owned our house before we did.

But it was only after Jack's death that my dream began to take shape. As I struggled to put the pieces of my life back together, I remembered that conversation and started getting estimates to convert the long-deserted cottage into my office and my shop.

The name came to me like a ray of sunshine one spring day when I was planting bright orange marigolds along my patio. My shop would be called Marigold's. It was a happy name. A name that promised sunshine and abundance. Out came Jack's yellow legal pads—and, of course, a few tears. I began to outline ideas, and gradually found that it made me very happy to move forward. The sight of those legal pads brought back so many memories of Jack holding not one, but several, legal pads as he took endless notes about his cases, his career plans, and our plans for the future. Now the pads chronicled my progress as my future began taking shape.

For some reason, the bright sunshine and bright marigold blooms triggered dusty memories this morning. Those wonderful, terrible, happy, tragic memories continued to parade around my mind, even ten years after Jack died in a senseless car accident. And those memories continued to cause a surge of anger whenever I thought of the young drunk driver who had killed a wonderful man. My handsome, funny, caring husband. That drunk driver made me a widow. That drunk driver robbed my life of the possibility of having children. He robbed me of more joy than I could possibly comprehend.

I still found the tragedy unbelievable when I was alone late at night. "Grief knows no timetable," the therapist told me months after the accident, as I continued to grieve. Ten years later, even the sunniest, most promising day was both happy and sad. I loved my business, but I could easily feel a tear slide down my cheek when I saw a beautiful leather watch band on a man's wrist. That was my graduation gift to Jack. Knowing that the world of law is all about billable hours, I had wanted a special gift for my special lawyer. Neither Jack nor his watch survived the trip to the hardware store that day.

My Monday was well under way when I heard the tinkle of the bell on the shop door announcing my first customer of the day. I looked up and smiled at the middle-aged lady who walked through the door. She told me she was looking for an oak library table for her entry hall. An hour later, she was scheduling the delivery of a Windsor bench for her living room and a pair of very pretty gold-framed mirrors for a space yet to be determined. When I returned her credit card, she noticed my Friendship Board, which has a prominent place on the wall and the list of classes posted.

"I love this idea!" she said, peering at the smiling faces and funny notes sent from customers after they get home with a Marigold's treasure. And the class pictures taken during my design and gardening programs. And notes from friends chronicling their journeys. In fact, the Friendship Board is so popular that I've started a new version: clients send pictures of a special antique they hope to find or a space they'd like to redecorate or a plot of land they hope to transform into a garden. After I think about options and resources, we meet or skype and arrange face time. A whole new version of Marigold's business is emerging as technologies change the way I do business.

By noon, I started getting ready for class. The ancient pine farm table is surrounded by eight mismatched chairs, all painted a different color, thanks to Anna. On the worn table surface, I set the green Depression glass plates, and several pitchers of sweet tea and a platter of lemon bars and chocolate brownies. I ran my hands across the table's old stains and the carvings on the top, appreciating the patina as I imagined the craftsman who built the table and the people who enjoyed sitting around the table through the years. I love it.

Some children must have done their homework on the wooden tabletop, or played board games there, and whole families must have eaten countless meals around its broad expanse. I found this piece at an auction years ago. Instantly, I knew it would become the centerpiece for my classroom. When classes don't congregate here, I use it when I unpack boxes, set up displays, or host a "planning retreat." And twice a year, Ellie and I sit down here together and discuss ways we can further develop our businesses.

In fact, it was here that I suggested Ellie expand Annabelle's Bakery to become Annabelle's Bakery & Café. Ellie liked the idea. She transformed the old, 1950s-style bakery her grandmother had owned into a trendy cafe offering egg scrambles, herb-filled omelets, an assortment of baked goods, and mouth-watering quiches. Six days a week, crowds line up in front of the registers or wait patiently to sit at the quaint café tables. The intoxicating aromas of cinnamon, ginger, nutmeg, and sugar hover over the long boards where Ellie and her staff create their master-pieces. And everything is served on an eclectic assort-ment of vintage mismatched dishes, most of which I found for Annabelle's. At one of our mini-retreats, Ellie decided to have Anna stencil the buff-colored walls with words of wisdom. The idea was a winner: it's fun to see people study and discuss the quotes that swirl around the café walls.

Just before time for my class to start, I heard a car door close. Peering out the porch window, I saw a tall, dark-haired man, probably in his early forties, wearing green scrubs hurrying up the walkway towards Marigold's.

"Good morning," I called after the bell jingled and he entered. I could see that my visitor was hold-ing a piece of notepaper in his hand as he walked up to the counter. He seemed to study me before he spoke. I looked back at him, feeling a hint of shyness.

"I'm glad you're open," he said, with what I thought was awkwardness.

"Yes, I am," I said. "I'm Meg. How may I help you?" When he didn't immediately answer, I prompted, "You look like you have a list." I smiled and nodded at what the handsome doctor was holding in his hand.

"Well," he said, clearing his throat and looking at the paper he was clutching. "My mother sent me over here with orders to choose a large platter for my sister's wedding gift. I think she might have called you." He grinned at me then, with a broad, warm smile.

I nodded. "Then I know who you are, Audrey Carter's son." When he returned my nod, I asked, "How is she doing? She told me she broke her ankle by tripping over the dog. Since it happened just before the wedding, I guess she must be feeling a bit—or more than a bit—overwhelmed."

"She certainly is," he said with a rueful grin. "At this moment, she is sitting on her patio with her leg propped up, busily handing out assignments." He laughed. "I thought I got off easy when she sent me here."

"Then we certainly shouldn't keep her waiting. She gave me some clues about what she hoped you'd find," I said, hurrying to the closet that served as my storeroom. "Let me get the platters I have in stock. From what your mother said, any of them will be perfect."

"Do I know you?" he asked, looking at me intently after I laid the four white ironstone platters in a row on the counter. "You look familiar. But I know that I've never been in this shop. In fact, I'm afraid to move—I'm dangerous when china and glass are around. And you sure have a lot of glassware here." He scanned the shop with interest—and a rueful look on his face.

I laughed again. "I must admit, when your mother called, she warned me that you were the proverbial bull in a china shop—and this can be considered a china shop!"

He grinned but didn't speak. Again, he seemed to study my face, waiting for me to reply to his question. I answered as casually as I could manage. "We might have passed each other on the street. Or in Annabelle's Bakery & Café. Savannah still is a small-town in that regard."

"Maybe," he said. But he didn't look convinced. He finally turned his attention to the task at hand, though. Glancing at the four platters, he said, "Thanks—you've saved me a lot of time and effort. Let's go with the largest platter. That should accommodate the biggest turkey my sister Amy will find here in Savannah—and I'm sure it will make her dinners memorable. Mom seems convinced that Amy cannot possibly get married without the satisfaction of knowing she has the perfect platter for her new home."

"That's a fine choice," I said, noticing that kept checking his watch. "Are you in a hurry?" I asked, pulling out a box and long sheet of orange tissue paper and orange ribbon.

"I'm on my way to work. The ER at Memorial Hospital," he said. "I'll just have a seat at the table, if that's okay, while you wrap." He pulled out his cellphone to check his texts as soon as he sat. "By the way, I'm DOC," he said over his shoulder.

"Of course you are! I'll just be a minute, DOC," I said. "That is certainly an easy name to remember, with your profession." I smiled, trying to cover my unease. Just the mention of an ER made me feel queasy.

"Are you okay?" He turned at my words and must have noticed my hands shaking.

"I am, thanks, "I stammered. " It's just that, well…never mind." I bent over the wrapping, so my face was hidden.

"Bad experience?" he asked.

"Yes. Really, really bad," was all that I could manage to say.

Possibly to divert my thoughts, he set his phone down and offered, "Actually, my name is Denton Owen Carter, but as a kid I got the nickname from my initials. When I decided to go to med school, the name stuck. Or maybe I went to med school because of the name." he chuckled.

And then, as he was talking to me, I saw a change in his expression, and I realized that he remembered who I was too. My pixie-ish choppy haircut and chocolate brown eyes hadn't changed much over the past decade. Yes, I was the wife of the young lawyer killed by the drunk driver years ago. DOC had been on duty that day, the first to reach the bloodied man on the stretcher who had arrived in an ambulance with a screaming siren. The trauma surgeon was the one who told me that Jack was dead, but I was sure DOC could vividly remember my anguished cries at the news. He had tried to console me, just before Ellie wrapped her arms around me.

In fact, DOC had been called to testify at the trial, where I sat like a stone statue listening to the tragic story of a promising young man celebrating his college graduation with way too much drinking and partying. His big SUV had hurtled through the red light going twice the speed limit. Jack's little black sports car didn't stand a chance. Jack Kingston's life was taken from him by a bright young man who should have known better. The driver's life was ruined, too, of course. He had been sent to prison instead of law school. It was the classic story of someone who was not a bad person doing a bad thing.

During the course of the trial, I learned that nearly half—forty-five percent, to be exact—of all car accidents are linked to alcohol. As a trial lawyer and lobbyist, Jack had been making a career of getting alcoholics off the road. But he was killed by a drunk driver who never should have been on the road. The irony of it was still too much for me to comprehend at times.

DOC didn't say anything about recognizing me. He paid for the platter, thanked me as he took the box with the bright orange bow out of my arms, He left Marigold's with a wave of his hand. He must have noticed how pale I had become during our conversation, I realized. My face felt ashen. I put my hands on my cheeks, as if to warm them, reminding myself to breathe deeply and calm down.

I had noticed DOC grabbing one of my business cards. He'd tucked it into his pocket while I was tying the bow on the package. I wondered why. He didn't look like one of my usual clients.

"Thanks, Meg," DOC called as he waked towards the door.

"Be sure to tell Audrey hello and wish her a speedy recovery," I said, following him onto the porch.

And then I saw his black BMW parked on the street. Old memories flooded through me.

I hurried back into the shop, took a deep breath, and finished preparing for my kitchen design class and the ladies who were due to arrive soon. I put a pad of paper, pen, and handouts at each of the eight places around the farm table.

I didn't hear a car drive up, but a lady in a floral skirt and gauzy blouse entered Marigold's as I finished my preparations.

"Hello!" she called as soon as she entered the shop. Somehow, she seemed to radiate joy.

"Just what I need! A happy customer," I told myself with relief.

"How may I help you?" I asked, smiling back at her.

"Well, I've heard about your shop and I just couldn't wait to come here. "

"I'm Meg, the owner of Marigold's. Welcome!" I saw her eyes scan the shop and asked, "Are you looking for anything specific or maybe a decorating class?"

A huge smile spread across her face. "Yes. White ironstone sugar bowls. And, by the way, I'm Susan."

"Well, what a fun collection!" I smiled again. "Ironstone is one of my specialties, and I just happen to have several for you to look at." Out of curiosity, I added, "Why sugar bowls?"

"You must hear all kinds of stories about collections," she said with excitement in her voice." I've lost over seventy pounds because I stopped eating sugar. So, I now collect sugar bowls."

I laughed with more joy than I had felt in a long time. "Oh, my! A big congrats to you! Let me show you some choices. I have several particular favorites for you to consider."

As I moved through the shop gathering the sugar bowls, Susan Chandler chatted more about the fun she was having adding to her collection. I immediately thought of my Friendship Board. "Do you mind if I take your picture and add you to my Friendship Board?" I asked. "Everyone will love your story."

"I'd be honored," my guest said. I quickly snapped her photo, but had no time for more conversation before Marigold's door opened again, and my students flooded my shop, chattering about kitchen renovations, dishes, vintage pottery manufacturers, mixing bowls, linens, and flatware. Susan pulled up an extra chair and entertained the group with her sugar bowl story at my request, as I wrapped several pieces for her.

"Do you mind if I join your class?" she asked when I handed her the package. She entered into our discussions about cabinetry, incorporating old and new, and the visual importance of countertops, among other topics.

"Countertops serve as an important focal point for every kitchen," I reminded the class, and then moved on to discuss the variety of options. When we discussed cabinetry, I showed examples of kitchens with and without glass doors on above-counter cupboards. "See how the glass doors seem to add space to a small kitchen?" I suggested. "They not only display your prettiest dishes and glassware, but they appear to extend the room."

From cabinets we moved on to discuss the pros and cons of using subway tiles in a kitchen. Then I spread photos of different vintage wardrobes and Hoosiers across the table. "For kitchens with less than optimal storage space, consider using antiques such as these," I told the class, showing how wardrobes could be made useful as a dish pantry by adding shelves.

CHAPTER 3

Tuesday

I was pricing several exceptional pieces of antique cherry furniture I had acquired at an estate sale when Ellie arrived early Tuesday morning with a woman I didn't know.

"Hi," I grinned at my best friend. "How is your day going?"

"Awesome," Ellie said, adding with a smile at the stranger, "And, I've brought you a new customer and friend. This is Jenny Thompson from Indianapolis."

I held out my hand and shook hers warmly. "Wow," I said, "that's quite a road trip! Welcome to Marigold's."

When she returned my handshake, we made small talk. "How did you two connect?" I asked.

Ellie handed me a vanilla latte and gestured to the farm table, where we all sat down. She pulled a bag of blueberry scones from her tote, and we were ready to chat. "Jenny was staying at the Ivy House Inn just down the street, and they directed her to Annabelle's for breakfast," Ellie said, all smiles. "I introduced myself, we started a conversation, and here we are at Marigold's."

"Well, I know enough about my best friend to know that she has something up her sleeve," I told Jenny. "I'm intrigued."

Jenny appeared to be in her mid-forties with short curly light-brown hair and eyes that seemed full of a wisdom and compassion far beyond her years. She was dressed in a cute denim skirt with a cotton tee-shirt and wedge sandals. She shared some of her life story as we drank our lattes on this gorgeous early spring day. A native of Indianapolis, she told us she had always dreamed of writing professionally and had just attended a writing conference in Atlanta. "I decided on a whim to rent a car to drive the three hours to Savannah instead of flying back to Indy yesterday," she explained.

"Savannah is where my mother was born, and her family lived here for generations," she said. "I decided to find a very special gift here to celebrate her seventieth birthday. I thought I might find something in Savannah that would remind her of her roots, her heritage."

"What a lovely thought! I'm sure we can find something that she will love, Jenny." I scanned the treasures that I was displaying on shelves, tables, and countertops. "Does your mom have a special interest in antiques or garden items? Or, maybe, both?" I inquired.

"Well, she loves to entertain. I was thinking of looking for a beautiful cut-glass cake plate for her birthday party."

"That's a beautiful, thoughtful, and useful idea," I said, wandering around the shop in search of possibilities. "And, while we're at it," I added, "you've given me a story to add to my Friendship Board."

"You've got to see this Friendship Board," Ellie invited, beckoning Jenny over to the collection of smiling photos and stories that I proudly displayed behind the sales counter.

"I'd be honored to have my story join these others," Jenny said, studying the entries one by one.

Before I could join them at the Friendship Board, in bounced Anna. My best friend's daughter is a Mini-me Ellie. Both have the same sparkling blue eyes and wavy blond hair. On this day, Anna had tied her long ponytail back with some kind of tie-dyed ribbon. Ellie, a very busy baker, wore her blond hair in a chin-length blunt cut, with the sides flipped behind her ears.

"I just dropped by to bring Lucy a new collar," Anna announced as she pulled a bright purple piece of leather studded with pearls out of her huge shoulder bag. She headed in the direction of my gray cat.

Ellie and I laughed. Anna had been dressing Lucy since she brought her to me not long after Jack died. It really is quite a story. Only a few months after the funeral, Ellie's little girl walked into my kitchen one morning with a big straw tote bag on her little shoulder. I heard a tiny meow and looked at Anna for clarification, but all I saw was Anna grinning from ear to ear.

"I don't want you to live alone, Meg," she told me, reaching carefully into her bag. "So when I heard that my friend Tessa's cat had kittens that were old enough to go to new homes, I went and chose the very prettiest one for you." She held her selection out to me and asked, "Isn't she the sweetest thing you ever saw?"

"Does your mom know about this?" I asked.

"She just knows that I walked over to visit you," she said. But of course there was nothing unusual about this. Anna was allowed to walk the one short block between our houses—and she did so frequently.

"Well," I said, "let me think about this." I was still in a state of shock, barely able to decide what to eat for dinner, let alone capable of making any changes in my home life. I wasn't prepared for the tiny gray ball of fur, even if she was beyond adorable.

But Anna just kept smiling at me, watching me intently with those compelling blue eyes. "Okay," I conceded at last, after taking a deep breath, "but only if you agree that we'll take care of her together."

"It's a deal, Meg," she said, depositing the tiny fluff ball into the palm of my hand.

"Do you have a name in mind?" I asked.

"Yes, I do! And I know you'll love it," she said happily.

"Well, I'm sure I will," I said, returning her smile with one of the first smiles I'd been able to muster since the funeral. "What is it?"

"Well, you know how we watch *I Love Lucy* re-runs so we can…well, you know…laugh again? I decided we should call her Lucy. It's is a perfect name, don't you think?"

Once again, I was astounded at the wisdom of my little therapist and the startling intuition she applied in helping me come to grips with my new life.

My godchild managed to amaze me every single day. And on this particular day, she had outdone herself.

"Well, little Lucy," I said to the kitten, holding her up so we were on an eyes-to-eyes level. "That is the perfect name for you. And I know you'll bring your friend Anna and me as much joy as your name-sake has."

I turned and hugged the little girl tightly. "I can't thank you enough, little Miss Anna," I said fighting back the tears.

"And that's how Lucy came into my life after Jack died," I said, telling Jenny the story as Anna chased Lucy around the shop.

"Anna," said Jenny, "my boys, Sam and Seth, would love you. They're twins, and they spent their boyhood bringing me every stray cat and dog for miles around. Of course, they would fight over you. How do you feel about older men? They're twenty years old now, students at Indiana University."

We all laughed. Anna gathered her backpack and purse before preparing to head to class at Savannah College of Art and Design. I told Jenny that SCAD had turned out to be the perfect art school for Anna's vibrant personality. "Anna planned to become an artist from the days when she was a tiny girl with her first box of watercolors," I told Jenny proudly. "Anna has always had a plan for everything." I laughed.

"Oh, Meg, you're making me blush!" Anna said, smiling at me as she moved toward the door.

After wishing Anna a good day, I turned to Jenny and asked her to tell us about her writing.

She explained that her love for reading and writing went back to her early childhood, so she majored in creative writing when she was a student at Butler University in Indy. "My first teaching job was in a high school and before and after school, I spent my time writing short stories, though never for publication," she said.

A life-changing event that happened a few years earlier had caused her to focus more seriously on her writing. "I was diagnosed with breast cancer," she told us, unconsciously running her hand across her chest. "I had to take a leave from school, and the hours at home were long and often lonely. I wrote stories to get my feelings on paper, and the process was so rewarding that I decided not to return to the classroom, but to keep focused on writing."

She explained that she was working on her first book, yet to be titled, based on her experience with cancer and recovery. "I signed up for the Atlanta Writing Conference to learn more about the craft and my new, second career," she said. "I've fallen in love with the power of words and the way my thoughts and experiences can reach out to people I've never met. It was an excellent conference," she said.

"But enough about me," she added quickly. "I'd really love to hear about both of you, if you have time."

I smiled at her and gave a brief overview of how Jack and I had bought the lovely but very outdated house with the small stone cottage in the bak yard. We were ready to plan renovations while we both started our careers. "But, in an instant, my life changed radically when he was killed by a drunk driver," I told her. "I closed my interior design firm to reorient myself. Months later, I decided that I truly loved the field. Although I still wanted to work for myself, I wanted to give myself the opportunity to take my business in a new direction. This old stone cottage was just sitting here, waiting for me to turn it into my new office, a classroom, and a welcoming, intriguing shop filled with antiques and collectibles."

"You've certainly done that," Jenny agreed, her eyes roaming around the shop.

"She really has. We're very proud of Meg's accomplishments," Ellie added.

I told Jenny what Ellie knew: that the garden I planted and expanded and loved was not just a labor of love, but a place where I—and others—could find peace and so much more. But I decided to save the rest of that story for later. "On to you, Ellie," I invited.

Ellie described how, as young girls, we had both helped her Grandmother Annabelle in her bakery, aptly called Annabelle's. "Mark and I married right after college," she said. "When sweet little Anna came along, we named her for my precious grandma. I had returned to teaching, but when grandma became ill and died, she left the bakery to me. I discovered that my inheritance was a very special gift—as well as a new career direction for me. Anna has grown up at Annabelle's just as Meg and I did." Ellie said.

Ellie described the way she had expanded the business by adding a cafe with breakfast and luncheon menus that changed regularly. "Anna works in both shops, to help us and to earn extra money when she isn't in class," Ellie explained. "She has a real gift for customer service."

"As well as a loving spirit and amazing talent in creative arts," I added. "In fact, Anna is one of the rare artists who can list 'business savvy' on her resume."

Before we knew it, the time had slipped away, and late-afternoon shadows were tiptoeing into my garden. With advice from us, Jenny chose a beautiful footed cut-glass cake plate, which I wrapped. Long before I tied the bright orange bow on top, we all agreed that it seemed like we had known each other forever. As I added Jenny's story to my Friendship Board, both Ellie and I told our new Indianapolis friend that creating new friendships had become a big part of why we both love our businesses.

CHAPTER 4

Wednesday

It was another idyllic day in Savannah as Jenny left the nearby Inn and I left my home, both of us walking half a block to Annabelle's Bakery & Café, to choose another selection from the extraordinary breakfast menu.

When the bell jingled over the café door, Ellie looked up and made her way through the crowd to show Jenny the last available table. I joined her there, in time to hear Jenny tell Ellie that she was dropping her original plan, which had been to start the drive home early that morning. "I'm going with Plan B," she said, "which I made after leaving you and Meg yesterday. I decided to call Mom and invite her to fly down to Savannah and show me the special places of her childhood city."

Jenny told us that her mother, whose name was Karen Ashland, had said, "I had no idea you cared to tour my old hometown."

"I knew by the catch in her voice that she was very pleased," Jenny added. "She didn't hesitate to agree to meet me here. I decided to wait until the drive from the airport to tell Mom about my two new friends here."

Jenny looked a little sheepish when she admitted she wasn't sure she could explain exactly why she was drawn so strongly to Savannah and its people. "Maybe it's my family's roots here—roots that were almost lost to me," she suggested. "Anyway, I told Mom, " Let's explore Savannah together, and we can drive back when we feel like it." she said.

"Well, we certainly enjoyed meeting you, and we'll look forward to meeting your mother," Ellie told Jenny. "I truly believe this old city has something special that draws people into its inner circle and convinces them to stay and become better acquainted."

Jenny agreed. Seeing the waitress approach, she scanned the menu and admitted she couldn't make up her mind about the selections, so Ellie prompted, "What about the special today? An omelet with brie cheese, diced tomato, mushrooms and fresh basil, served with fresh fruit and buttered sourdough toast? Or, maybe the oatmeal with blueberries and walnuts? Then again, you might want something lighter: whipped eggs with parmesan cheese and parsley?"

"All three, please. And I'm never going home because I won't be able to move from my chair," Jenny laughed.

"The servers will be here to take your order in a moment when you positively make up your mind," Ellie smiled. "And, now that I think of it, you've given me a good idea! Maybe I should offer a sample platter of three choices."

After breakfast, Ellie waved goodbye to us and Jenny accompanied me to Marigold's, with a tote bag full of notebooks and pens. While I unlocked my shop door, she settled into a rocker on the porch, describing her favorite townhouses we had passed together that morning. "I absolutely love the miniature gardens, courtyards, and patios I glimpsed through wrought-iron fences," she said.

"I'm going to grab a bottled water. Do you want one?" I asked.

She thanked me and added, "I hope you don't mind, but I thought I'd sit here and do some writing. Maybe I'll try to sketch your house, although I'm not really an artist."

"Have fun writing and drawing! And, I'll just be inside if you need me," I invited.

Later that morning, glancing over Jenny's shoulder, I saw sketches of my two-story stone house from two directions. The front sketch showed the black shutters, wide porch, and front door (which is the color of celery) with the little "WELCOME" sign hanging in its center. Jenny had even drawn the wrought-iron hay-rack planters that hung beneath the first-floor windows. Weeks earlier, I filled them with red geraniums, white petunias and long vinca vines.

The second sketch showed the side of my house and the door leading to the side porch. Jenny was in the process of drawing the trees, shrubs, and birdbath in the garden when I brought her a cold water. She had already drawn the wide stepping stones and pea gravel winding through the gardens to the stone cottage. I glanced up to compare the sketch to the reality. The garden that linked the house and shop was lush with shade trees, blooming azaleas, hearty rhododendron bushes, elegant magnolias, flowers representing all the colors in a rainbow, and a kitchen garden crowded with varieties of herbs. Jenny had done an excellent job of capturing its features.

"It looks as though you placed the Adirondack chairs by the old oak tree with an artist's eye," Jenny said, continuing to sketch. "And the tables surrounded by chairs seem to invite groups of friends to visit, relax, and enjoy the serenity."

"I'm glad you think so," I said.

"What is it about this place that makes me feel so peaceful?" Jenny asked as she continued to sketch.

"Well, I'll have to think about that for a moment, I guess," I suggested, changing the subject to give myself time to think. "Jenny, when does your mother arrive?"

"Two o'clock this afternoon," Jenny said, adding, "I am so very glad I changed my plans. A mother-daughter vacation is just what we both need—and now that Mom's retired and I've changed my career, we have time for something fun. I think Mom will love the chance to become reacquainted with her hometown. Also, I'd like her to meet you and Ellie."

Jenny told me more than she had the day before, how her mother's family had left Savannah abruptly when Karen was only ten years old, after her father's company transferred him to a new job in Indianapolis. They never came back, despite their family's roots here.

"I told mom that I've found something very special about this place and its people, something that she needs to experience for herself," Jenny said. "She's a retired rehab nurse, so she's free to travel. In fact," she added, looking at her watch. "She should be climbing on her plane just about now."

"That's great," I said. "I have several meetings this afternoon, but I'll be back early. We can check with Ellie about her schedule, but I'd love to have you bring your mom here around five. Let's have sweet tea and hors d'oeuvres in the garden. Will that work for you?"

"Oh, that is too much trouble," Jenny protested. "But I do want you to meet Mom."

"It will be no trouble at all. Ellie and I will enjoy meeting your mother and letting her know about all the special places in her hometown that she might want to visit. Ellie and I chatted after work yesterday and we both agreed we feel like we've found a very special new friend in you. I can't explain it, but I appreciate it. Please come."

"In that case, we'd be honored—and we'll look forward to it," Jenny said. As I turned back to the store, she asked, "Do you mind if I sit in the garden and write until I have to leave for the airport?"

"Please do! I want you to enjoy it," I said. "Those lavender and lemon balm plants have such calming properties. I hope they'll inspire you. It seems to have become a healing garden." I smiled. "See you at five!"

Later that afternoon, Jenny climbed into her rental car and drove away from Marigold's, to meet her mother at the airport. She must have headed directly back, because I saw them wandering through my gardens on my walk back home from the shop. From what Karen Ashland told me when she was introduced, Jenny spent the entire drive talking about her new friends in Savannah. When I led the two ladies through the garden to my favorite spot, Karen told me, "My daughter really seems to have found some very special new friends. I've never seen her this excited about an adventure. And I'm so pleased to be back here in Savannah, with the chance to meet new friends."

"Good heavens, what did she tell you?" I asked, laughing, just as Ellie joined us, her arms laden with a tray containing a chilled pitcher of sweet tea and four of my antique glasses. She was just in time to hear the answer.

"That these two gifted businesswomen are enjoying wonderful, exciting careers and an even more wonderful friendship," Jenny said. Then she confessed a thought that made me pause. "There is something special about all this. I just can't explain it."

Neither could I.

Then, at least.

"You know, Meg, as we drove down your street, I recognized one of the homes," Karen told me. "Then I started really studying the neighborhood. I know this street. I know it very well. I even knew your house once upon a time."

"Really?" I asked, curious and hopeful I might learn something about the previous owners of my home.

"Yes," Karen answered. "I grew up on this street. My best friend, Patty Palmer, lived four houses down from me. When Jenny pulled up to the curb in front of your house, I asked her why she was stopping here, when she couldn't possibly know my connection to this place."

"You have a connection here?" I asked.

"She does!" Jenny said, excitedly. "I told her that this was your house, Meg, and that behind it is the shop named Marigold's that I'd been telling her about. You'll never guess the coincidence. It really is a small world."

"It is?" I asked.

"This is my dearest friend's house. This is Patty's old house. I would know it anywhere," Karen said. "When Jenny stopped outside your home, I pointed to the built-in benches that flank the front door and instantly remembered them. I recognized the house because of those benches. Patty and I used to play on them by the hours."

"Well, that is certainly strange," I said slowly as Ellie poured iced tea adding a sprig of mint from my garden in the tall glasses and I arranged plates of hors d'oeuvres. "What a small world this is!"

"This garden is breathtakingly lovely," Karen said, momentarily distracted. She bent to sniff a lavender plant.

"Yes, it is," Jenny agreed.

I was admiring Karen's spring-green wrap dress when she bent down, and I noticed something that made me gasp in surprise. The necklace Karen was wearing took my breath away. It was identical to the necklace my little-girl ghost Lovey wore, the same half-heart I saw in my mirrors whenever I glanced her way. What could that possibly mean?

I started to ask Karen about her necklace, but I couldn't decide what to say. Should I confess that I had a resident ghost and the ghost had something in common with Karen? Or would my new friends—and my oldest friend—think I was crazy?

"Stay calm. Wait and see," I mumbled to myself under my breath. To my guests, I suggested, "Please, sit down and help yourself to a glass of tea and something to eat."

We gathered around my garden table, talking and laughing. We all became acquainted on a new level, and the stories started to flow. In time, however, I noticed how often Karen kept looking at the big oak tree beside my shop.

"So, Karen," I said, trying subtly to change the direction of the conversation, "what a coincidence that you lived on this very street, and your best friend lived here, in my house." I told her how Jack and I had fallen in love with the house—which back then needed a lot of love and attention—and so we bought it as newlyweds. "I knew this house had a rich history over the last one hundred or more years, but I don't know anything about that history. Your visit is really special in several ways. Can you tell me about your friend and anything you might know about this place?" I asked.

I saw tears glistening in Karen's eyes as she took a deep breath. Finally she took a sip of her tea and started a story that caused Jenny, Ellie, and me to lean forward and hold our collective breath so we wouldn't miss a word.

"There's much to tell, but I'll go straight to the most important day of my first ten years," Karen said. "It was a hot summer day. Patty and I went to the library to get new Nancy Drew books. And then we collected a bag of cookies and a thermos of cold lemonade and went to our favorite spot to enjoy them—that old tree over there." She pointed to the large oak tree beside Marigold's, whose wide-spreading branches reached over my garden and nearly to my shop.

Karen fixed her attention on the tree and paused before continuing, "Sometime years earlier, when Patty's brothers were small, her dad had built a great tree house that all of the neighbor kids had loved. " Again she interrupted her story to look at the ancient oak before turning her attention back to us.

"To get into the treehouse, we climbed narrow wooden steps," she explained. "We were almost to the top step when Patty started to drop the books. She reached out for them, caught her foot somehow, and lost her balance. I tried to catch her arm, but she slipped through my fingers. Instead, she grabbed onto the hem of my sundress as she fell."

Here Karen's voice broke, and she bowed her head for a moment before she continued, "As Patty fell, she pulled me down with her. I saw Patty hit her head just before I hit the ground and was knocked out. When I woke up in the hospital, I learned I had broken both of my legs. But, that wasn't the worst part. When I asked why Patty hadn't come to see me, I was told that Patty had died."

Jenny, Ellie, and I gasped simultaneously, staring at the white-faced woman. After a long pause, Karen continued her story. "I spent the entire summer in the hospital, but the news of Patty's death was beyond anything I could comprehend. My best friend had died. I hadn't been able to save her. We were only ten."

Long minutes passed before any of us could speak. Jenny, who must not have heard the story over the years, appeared to be as stunned as Ellie and I were. We all had tears running silently, unnoticed, down our faces.

With a quivering voice, I said, "I am so very sorry, Karen—and I'm shocked that a tragedy like that happened in my yard. I had no idea." She nodded, keeping her head down as she wiped her eyes.

I took a deep breath and, with a sudden suspicion and intuition, I asked, "Can you tell me about that darling necklace that you're wearing?"

Karen fingered the gold half-heart hanging from the thin chain. "Patty and I had just exchanged these friendship hearts a few days before the accident. We each had a half. That was what little girls—best friends—shared in those days. I have kept mine in my jewelry box all these years. When Jenny called me and asked me to come to Savannah, I pulled it out for the first time in sixty years and looked at it closely. I decided to wear it on my visit here, though I'm not exactly sure why. I remembered my mother telling me that Patty was buried wearing her half of the heart."

I glanced at Ellie. My best friend had never said she didn't believe my stories about Lovey, the little girl in the pink sundress and pigtails who wore a gold half-heart necklace, but I knew she wasn't a big believer in ghosts. However, now Ellie looked at me with her eyes wide open, as speechless as I was.

Should I tell Karen and Jenny about my resident ghost? That question went through my mind over and over again. But, I just wasn't ready. I wanted an idea of what the consequences would be before I was willing to risk telling the story.

So, instead, we changed the conversation to happier topics. We talked about the history of Savannah, then Annabelle's and Marigold's as we dined on my thick crab soup, crusty bread with warm brie cheese, and fresh strawberries dipped in chocolate. I couldn't prevent myself from asking one more question, however. "What happened to you after the accident, Karen?"

"I suffered through years of surgeries on my legs, but something good came from them all. They inspired me to start my career in orthopedic rehabilitation, to help others like myself," she said. "I told myself that my career should honor Patty, who didn't get the opportunity to recover and grow up to have a career, husband, and children. In those days, sixty or more years ago, head injuries that severe were almost always fatal."

She added, "My father was terribly concerned about the sadness that consumed us all during that tragic summer, so he convinced his company to transfer him to Indianapolis several months after my hospital release. He never offered to bring us back here, and I never asked to return. In fact, I never considered returning to Savannah until Jenny's call yesterday. But I certainly never forgot the summer that changed my life and ended Patty's life."

"What happened to Patty's family after she died?" I asked cautiously.

"A neighbor wrote my mother to say that they remained here for a few years, but eventually they sold the house. Patty had two teenaged brothers who were in high school when we were ten. When they prepared to head off to college, their parents decided to move. They told neighbors that the house had become too big." Karen paused, then said almost reluctantly, "I do know that the day after the accident, her dad and brothers tore every board off the tree-house and destroyed those steps. My mother said they worked in a frenzy and it was too hard for her to watch. My father offered to help them, but they said they needed to do the work themselves."

A small voice inside my head told me to leave the conversation there. So, I changed the subject. Instead, we talked about the plans Jenny and Karen had made to tour Savannah the next day. They both marveled at Savannah's beautiful old trees that dripped Spanish moss and the cobblestone streets that gave our city a unique background noise whenever a car passed my house. Ellie suggested that the mother and daughter ride the trolley around Savannah as they explored the oldest city in Georgia. "Of course you have to visit the local shops and sights," she said. "You'll find all kinds of interesting old homes to explore and shops filled with everything you can imagine."

Then, just when I thought we'd reached safe ground with the conversation, Karen said, "I still write to Mrs. Palmer—well, she likes to be called Miss Kate. She is Patty's mom."

A shocked silence greeted this announcement. "What?" I asked. "Is she still living? Is she here in Savannah?"

It turns out that Patty's mother was ninety-three years old and sharp as a tack, according to Karen. "She lives in an assisted-living apartment," Karen said. "I started writing to her the first summer of the accident. I couldn't go to the funeral, and I felt so badly about that. From the summer when I turned eleven, I've sent her a note every summer since then. I wrote her about school, getting married, having babies, work, my children's news, retirement, and funny things that have happened. But, I haven't seen her since I was ten. When Jenny asked me to come, I decided I should go see her while I'm here.

"Would you like to go with me?' she asked after moment, looking at all of us.

"Yes!" we said at the same time.

CHAPTER 5

Thursday

The entire week was full of warm sunshine and breezes that kept the humidity at bay. Ellie called me as I headed to Marigold's. Jenny and Karen were still sitting in Annabelle's, enjoying a three cheese and vegetable frittata, fresh fruit, and peach tea, Ellie informed me. She said that Karen had made a call to the assisted-living center. "She spoke to Miss Kate's nurse, who verified that Miss Kate could receive visitors," Ellie said. "Karen told the nurse that this was a special visit so she could prepare Miss Kate for meeting Karen and the rest of us," I could hear the excitement in my best friend's voice.

After breakfast, Jenny and Karen walked to Marigold's, to share the itinerary with me for the next day, when they planned to visit Miss Kate. Then Karen spent a good hour browsing through my collections, looking at everything lining the shelves and cabinets and hanging on the walls. Jenny once again had taken her pencils and notebooks to my porch and spent her time writing. They were just leaving when Anna parked her bright yellow VW and jumped out with a happy expression on her face. She was wearing a dress as vivid and full of sunshine as the car.

"This is Ellie's daughter, Anna—and my god-daughter," I said.

Jenny waved a hand, motioning towards the car, suggesting, "I bet there is a story there."

"Of course," I said with a smile, though I could feel a trace of sadness when I began my version. "Last year, when Anna turned eighteen, I surprised her with the car as a combination birthday and high school graduation gift. Jack always called Anna 'Sunshine,' for obvious reasons. She is so full of life and happiness—and she has been that way since she was born. So, I chose yellow, the color of sunshine, for her first car."

Karen and Jenny both smiled as Jenny told her mother, "Remember how I said there was something special about our new friends?"

Anna delivered Ellie's contributions to my cookie jar, hugged me, and hurried off to school after shaking hands with our two new friends. Following a few moments discussing their itinerary, Karen and Jenny headed off on their day of sightseeing and shopping. "We're going to eat lunch at that outside café down by the water—the one Ellie recommended," Jenny said. "I'm looking forward to their crab salad sandwiches."

By evening, they had returned to my garden. After I locked Marigold's door for the day and joined them on a bench overlooking the roses, Jenny announced she had an idea she hoped I would like. "I want to organize a writing retreat in Savannah," she said. "Specifically, in your garden, Meg. If, that is, you don't mind."

CHAPTER 6

Friday

I always feel a tingle of pleasure mixed with mystery when I know I'm bound for an adventure and a chance to make a new friend. Today was one of those days. This time when I awoke early, I didn't lie in bed. I jumped out of bed, showered, did a few quick chores, and waited impatiently for Jenny and Karen to arrive on my front porch. They appeared promptly at nine o'clock, as we had arranged. A few minutes later, Ellie and Anna pulled up to the curb to pick us all up. Excitement filled Ellie's tan Buick SUV as we headed to the other side of town and Miss Kate.

Ellie had packed a white baker's box with sugar cookies thickly frosted in pink icing and covered in sprinkles. Just after sunrise, I had picked a bouquet of lavender, red roses, daisies, Queen Anne's lace, and orange tiger lilies and arranged them in an old white ironstone pitcher. The riot of color was gorgeous, and the fragrances filled the car, causing us all to sniff appreciatively.

The assisted-living facility was a cheerful two-story brick building surrounded by flowering trees and gardens. Jenny, Ellie, Anna, and I went directly to the visitors' porch and waited while Karen went to Miss Kate's room to greet her. After a few minutes, they joined us on the porch.

At ninety-three years young, Miss Kate was the most precious lady I had ever met. She was wearing cream-colored linen slacks and a royal blue blouse that reflected the color of her eyes, which were surrounded by smile lines. Her short silver-gray hair was pulled back with silver combs. She clapped her hands together and smiled when she was introduced to us, but her eyes sparkled with tears—and we knew they were tears of joy.

We all took turns hugging her, trying not to overwhelm her. Introductions were made. Holding Miss Kate's hand, Karen started telling the story of her first trip back to Savannah, which started with Jenny's decision to drive to Karen's hometown in search of a cake plate. She described Jenny's first visit to Annabelle's and Marigold's, and then her own visits there. "And that is how these amazing new friendships began," she concluded.

Miss Kate asked how Ellie and I knew each other. We told the story together, laughing and finishing each other's sentences. And then, in a quivery voice, Miss Kate asked about my home—her former home.

I described its appearance fifteen years ago, when Jack and I first laid eyes upon our dream home, and I described the work and many projects that had gradually transformed it. Anna, always the glue that binds all of us together, moved over to Miss Kate and held her other hand. "Let me tell you more about Meg's home," she suggested, and we all relaxed.

Anna talked about her early memories of visits to see Jack and me. She said how much she loved me— "I call her my other mom," she said. "And I adored Jack." She told Miss Kate about Jack's tragic death ten years earlier, when she was nine. She told her about having her own room upstairs in my house and about the little slumber parties we regularly held there. She described Lucy, our cat, and how we came to name her. Last of all, she described my special garden.

"Why is it special? " Miss Kate asked.

"Well, it's hard to describe. It's beautiful—but that doesn't describe the way it makes you feel when you sit there," Anna said, with a dreamy look in her eyes. She squeezed Miss Kate's hand. "You'll have to experience it for yourself, I guess."

Then Miss Kate said, "I'm so grateful for your visit. I want to share my special album with you. I don't show many people this album, but I'd like you to see it. Karen, could you please go back to my room and get it? It's the pink leather album on my night-stand. I left it out, hoping that I could show it to you."

"Of course," Karen said. She immediately headed to Miss Kate's room and returned with a well-worn album. When Miss Kate started her story, we were all stunned.

She smiled at Karen and said, "I can't begin to thank you for all that you've done for me over the last sixty years. I have had the privilege to live part of my life through you, as if my precious Patty were still here, alive and having marvelous adventures." And then she opened the album. We sat speechless listening to her as she turned the pages.

"Karen and Patty were the best of friends," she began, nodding to Karen. "Those girls became so much a part of each other's families that it must have been almost like living in two houses for them. They truly were inseparable little girls, the very best of friends—and not many of us can claim a friendship like theirs." She nodded at Ellie and me. "I think you two understand that kind of friendship."

We glanced at each other, smiled, and nodded.

Miss Kate turned another page of the album and we saw photographs of two happy little girls playing together, laughing together, wearing matching outfits, and posing with broad smiles on their faces. As the elderly woman turned the next page, we saw a picture of my oak tree—looking much younger—and two little faces peering from the branches.

Miss Kate ran her finger over the picture before saying to Karen, "That afternoon when you both fell off the top rung of the tree house ladder and I ran screaming to the foot of the tree, I thought my life was over. I was just flatten by grief. I had a husband and two teenaged sons who still needed me, but it was you that I needed after I buried my precious little girl. I was desperate for you to recover that long summer. You were injured so badly, both physically and emotionally. Too young at ten to understand any of it. Then, later, when your dad was transferred and you moved to Indiana, I felt as if I were losing my daughter all over again."

Karen's eyes filled with tears and she squeezed Miss Kate's hand before the elderly woman continued her story. "I was beyond thrilled to get your first letter after you moved. But my real surprise has been that every year since then, sixty years to be exact, you have written me about yourself, your family, and your career. I've lived vicariously through you, as if knowing you meant I could know my Patty as a grownup." She finished with a soft meaningful smile and a faraway look in her eyes.

"Mom," Jenny said, "I didn't know all of this. I knew that you had a childhood friend who died, and that is why I was named Jennifer Patricia, but I didn't know about Miss Kate. Why didn't you tell me?"

Karen smiled ruefully at her daughter. "Well, it was such a long time ago. I have always held Patty very close to my heart. It's hard to tell a child about another child falling, hitting her head, and dying. You knew of the accident and my leg injuries and the years of surgeries and therapies. I always intended to tell you more details at some point, but the time just never seemed right. Your dad, of course, knows it all."

As Miss Kate continued to page through the album, the years of Karen's life flowed past us for review. We saw grade school pictures of Karen, letters in childlike print, photographs of teenage proms, scenes from her college days, scenes from her career in rehab nursing, her wedding photograph, and, of course, Jenny's birth announcement and baby pictures. The photographs continued right up to Jenny's sons' graduations. We all smiled, laughed, and cried throughout the unexpected and unbelievable visit with Miss Kate.

At long last, we noticed that our elderly friend was looking weary. We stood to leave, but first I invited Miss Kate to lunch in my garden the next day and a tour of her old home.

"I'm so grateful, my dear," she exclaimed. She quickly accepted the invitation.

Anna leaned over and gave Miss Kate a kiss on her cheek. "I'll see you tomorrow," she promised, adding, "and maybe, if it's okay, I'll come visit you here sometimes. My grandmother lives out of state, and I miss her."

Miss Kate had fresh tears again when she said, "It would be my pleasure. My sons both live out of state also, and I don't have a granddaughter, just grandsons, so I need you."

Ellie and I just grinned at each other as Anna was just herself once again.

"I cannot thank you enough for the chance to catch up on sixty years," Karen said, wiping her eyes with a lacy handkerchief that Miss Kate handed to her. Jenny put her arm around her mother's shoulder and said, "We enjoyed it as much as you did—and we all learned something important today."

Ellie drove us all to my house. We went our separate ways with a heart full of memories to process.

That afternoon, I had a class to teach: everything anyone wanted to know about herbs, growing herbs, cooking with herbs, and the other benefits herbs offer, so I started getting ready for it immediately. Ellie returned to the bakery in time to greet the late lunch crowd. Anna slid behind the wheel of her mother's car, offering to drop Karen and Jenny off at one of the squares to catch a trolley to tour another section of our historic city. I walked home from Annabelle's with a smile on my face.

CHAPTER 7

Saturday

I spent the early morning in my shop, working on inventory and preparing for two home visits and several presentations over the next week, but by late morning I was in my kitchen preparing lunch for my guests. Cucumber soup. A salad of greens topped with diced apples, walnuts, and goat cheese, served with poppy seed dressing. Hot chicken shrimp pot pie. Ellie, I knew, would create something delicious for dessert.

Karen and Jenny stopped by briefly before heading to the Assisted Living, to chauffeur Miss Kate. Ellie arrived with a mouthwatering pie. Anna set the table in the garden with my collection of white ironstone and antique cutlery. Small white lights twinkled throughout the garden, despite the fact that it was broad daylight, giving it a shimmery, festive atmosphere. The flowers on my table and in the garden were so fragrant they seemed intoxicating. I was carrying out a frosty pitcher of sweet tea when my guests arrived.

"Sit here, Miss Kate, in the place of honor, so you can see the house and the garden," I suggested after we all hugged.

We had decided to settle down to lunch and more conversation before touring the house. Despite her obvious pleasure in the lunch, I noticed that Miss Kate kept looking towards the big oak tree. "I'm so sorry, Miss Kate," I said, presuming the sight was upsetting her. "Perhaps we should move our lunch into the dining room."

"No, of course not," she said quickly. "Of course I know the tree is there. I lived here a couple of years looking at that tree after my Patty died. I was just thinking about her, the special way she called me 'Mama' and climbed onto my lap at the end of the day, or if something happened to upset her. I'm marveling at the irony of meeting all of you here at my old house, and I'm marveling at the way this all came about because of Jenny and Karen. It's quite a story to absorb at my age."

"Yes," we all said at the same time. I noticed Karen squeezing Miss Kate's hand under the table.

When Ellie served us fresh raspberry pie with a dip of French vanilla ice cream, Miss Kate asked me to tell her about my garden.

"Well, as you may remember," I said, motioning to the space behind the house. "This yard was all grass between the house and the little stone cottage. When Jack and I moved in, we sat under that oak shade tree and planned all of the renovations for the house. Then I told him I wanted a little herb and kitchen garden. He laughed. You know, in those days as a new bride, I could barely boil water, so I imagine he thought gardening was a challenge bigger than the two of us."

"You've come a long way," they all said together, smiling.

"First, you have created a little paradise and secondly, you served us a magnificent lunch in this special setting," Miss Kate said. "Both require a lot of work."

I nodded, explaining, "The year after Jack died, I read lots of books about the soothing effects of gardening as I tried to get my life back on track. I started with a kitchen organic garden—leaf lettuce, onions, tomato plants, and a few herbs—parsley, rosemary, dill, and basil. I sat in this garden by myself late into the night many, many evenings, trying to deal with my pain. Gradually I began looking to the future, and I took out a piece of paper and outlined the restoration of the cottage and exactly how I wanted to design the interior and the surrounding gardens."

I confessed that learning to cook took years. "My goal was to cook and garden almost as skillfully as Ellie bakes. Those challenges all saved me during the dark days after Jack died. They actually helped heal me from the overwhelming grief. My little home and garden are like old trusted friends."

"Tell her the rest of the story," Anna prompted.

I smiled at her before glancing at Karen, Jenny, and Miss Kate. "I was beyond devastated, I missed Jack so much. So I decided to talk to a therapist. She was amazing and gave me some excellent advice, which I followed faithfully. She said that I should write down my feelings, both good and bad, in order to embrace the wonderful memories. And to document what I was having trouble letting go of, so I could bury them and move on."

During the course of my research into gardening, I told them, I planted my first rose bushes and lavender plants—"because the roses are so breathtakingly beautiful that they inspired me to focus on all the sources of beauty in the world, and the smell of lavender has been proven to relieve stress—by scientists and by me."

I told them that whenever I planted perennials, I placed the scraps of paper from my notes in the ground with the finest plants I could find. "The process became almost a spiritual healing for me," I explained. "I learned that grief has no timetable. I came to feel comfort and even joy in my garden."

I hesitated, but because these were friends, I confessed that I often sat in the garden at the end of the day talking to Jack, telling him my plans about opening Marigold's, discussing my master gardening classes, and, of course, reporting on whatever Anna was doing at the moment.

"I came to think of the garden as a burial ground for all bad and sad thoughts, and a place that could produce good and happy thoughts," I said. "A simple, but effective, source of joy for me. This became a healing garden. Over the years, the garden has grown and spread. It attracts families of birds and butterflies and honey bees. I've added more chairs and benches, so I could invite my customers and friends to pause here for a few minutes to enjoy the sights, sounds, smells, and the peace this place offers."

I pointed to a yellow rose bush with little buds. "Do you see that over there?"

Miss Kate nodded.

"Well last year, I was just closing my shop one evening when I saw a lady who is a frequent customer coming up the walk. She carried a shovel, the rose bush, and a smile on her face. I watched from the window as she walked into the garden and headed right to that spot. She started to dig and firmly settled the rose bush into the hole before shoveling dirt back around the base. I waited until she left before visiting the newest addition to my garden. Neither of us ever said a word until one afternoon, when I found her sitting near the rose bush, staring at it.

"I can't begin to tell you how much support you and your garden have been to me," she said, never taking her eyes off the roses.

"Please tell me," I said softly.

"I've often sat a few minutes in your garden over the last couple of years when I came to shop," she said, explaining that her mother's mind was declining from Alzheimer's disease. "I would always find comfort here," she said. "Mother recently passed, and in her honor I wanted to plant this yellow rose bush, her favorite variety."

Suddenly she looked at me, and I saw her cheeks turn red. "I hoped others would enjoy its beauty. I never gave a thought to the idea that you wouldn't approve."

"That story is as beautiful as your rose bush," I told her. "You were right. This is a fitting place to honor your mother. You're welcome to sit here anytime you need comfort.

"And," I added, 'Did you know that yellow roses are a sign of friendship?' We hugged. No other words were necessary."

"I totally understand where she was coming from." Jenny spoke softly, for the first time since our conversation turned to the garden. She told us all about her breast cancer detection, surgery, and recovery, her new writing career, and the urge to reach out to others in a new way, as an author. She turned to me and reintroduced the topic she had broached the night before.

"This is such a special place," she said. "I feel more inspired, less distracted, and more creative here than I've felt anywhere else. Meg, I'd like to talk to you about returning sometime soon with three other writing friends. With your permission, I'd like to plan a writing retreat, using your garden as our outdoor office. We could tour the city, eat at Annabelle's, and write in your garden.

"Would you approve of us sitting out here a few hours each day?" she asked me.

"Of course! You and your friends are always welcome." I said, speaking for Ellie and Anna, too. "We'd love to meet them and see you here often."

Jenny told us about her writing friends. They all live in an historic downtown neighborhood in Indianapolis. "They'll love Savannah, Marigold's, your amazing shop, this garden, and Ellie's cooking and baking," she said.

Jenny went on to discuss other plans for a stay in Savannah: maybe a day at a spa for pampering, daily yoga lessons, tours of the city, and walks along the quaint streets. "But predominantly, I want to plan it as a retreat, where we can write uninterrupted," she said. "These surroundings will promote that spirit."

She then talked about the friends she would invite. "One friend, Kim, is working on an anthology of nurses and their different careers, Lizzie has MS and is working on a non-fiction piece about chronic illness and Erica is writing a childrens book ," she said. "The four of us have been writing together since we met in a class a couple of years ago. Thanks to all of you, I may write about all the new friendships and exciting things that have happened on this journey. I'll record Mom's memories of Savannah, our family's roots here, Miss Kate, Patty, and, if I may, I'll write about you and Ellie. Old friends, new friendships. Those are priceless gifts, and I want to write about all of them."

"I can't think of a greater compliment," Ellie said, as Anna beamed.

"GIRLS, the friendship that we nurture, and the JOURNEY we travel together is priceless and time-less," I said smiling.

"Now, what about that tour of your house and Marigold's?" Anna prompted, standing up with an armful of dishes, which she carried to the kitchen. I took Miss Kate's arm and we all followed Anna into the house.

The kitchen was radically different from years past. Miss Kate studied the kitchen, commenting on the antique I'd converted into a kitchen island and the big picture window that now looked into the garden. "I love the room's old-fashioned charm—I'm certain the original builders would feel at home here, Meg," she said. She exclaimed at all of the other renovations on the main level. We didn't climb the stairs, but I described in detail the two sets of large, roomy bed-rooms that shared Jack-and-Jill bathrooms on each side of the stairs. But I didn't tell them that Jack and I had planned the layout for the four children we hoped to have.

I led my guests on a tour of the downstairs, through the large, sunny living room and dining room, both of them painted a shade of khaki that looked fresh and clean against the white crown mold-ing. They peeked into my small powder room whose walls were covered with framed antique floral prints, then proceeded on the way to my huge bedroom, a former owner's home office. This room had been added to the back of the house decades after the home was originally constructed. Jack and I converted it into a master bedroom with lots of closets, and a lux-urious bathroom. The bedroom walls had been a creamy white until the previous winter, when I decided on an entirely new look. I painted them the soft shade of ballet shoes, which seemed to wrap me in comfort whenever I spent time there.

"Jack and I chose this room for our first project and I really live on the first floor," I commented, as we returned to the kitchen. "But I'm happy to say that Anna and her friends frequently stay upstairs for sleepovers."

Then I got an idea. "Jenny, you and your friends could stay upstairs when you come, if you want," I offered. "You would each have a room and a shared bath, nothing special. But it would be a convenient place for you to stay, and it would certainly be close to the garden where you plan to do your writing. Plus,

I'd love to meet your friends and have a chance to get to know them—and you—better."

"That is beyond generous," Jenny said, hugging me. "Thank you! The girls will love it. Let's plan on it! You're sure it won't be inconvenient for you?"

When I shook my head, she thanked me again. "I'll talk to you about ideas as I plan the retreat," she promised. "Besides writing in this beautiful place, we could just sit outdoors and enjoy the garden late at night, reviewing what we'd written and offering each other advice." She listed the other benefits: "This is just a short walk over to Annabelle's, where we know breakfasts and lunches are marvelous. We could walk to breakfast, return here to write, take a break for lunch, and come back here to write again. Maybe I can arrange some sightseeing trips for the late afternoons, and we can explore the city's restaurants at night."

"You make everything sound so delightful! I might consider becoming a writer myself," I told Jenny, ushering my guests back to the garden.

On our walk through the garden to Marigold's, I noticed that Miss Kate starting smiling again. She nodded approvingly at the pots of plants and the green rocking chairs on the porch before stepping over the threshold and into my shop.

"I love this place," she said immediately. "Tell me all about it. I only went in here occasionally, when the children were using it for a rainy day clubhouse. What kind of work did it need?"

After I described the cottage's transformation, Miss Kate asked, "What made you go into interior design? What do you especially like about antiques?"

I talked about the collections I'd gathered for my home and garden, and the collections I offered for sale in Marigold's. "They link us to the past, and many come with intriguing stories that make their previous owners or makers come alive to me," I said. I told her about my classes , my love of white ironstone and the spirit of journey they inspired with old and new friends.

Soon, we could all tell that Miss Kate was tiring. Karen and Jenny offered to get their car while Miss Kate rested on the porch. When they arrived to drive her back to her home, we all hugged and promised to stay in touch.

And then something special happened. Extraordinary, really. When it became my turn for her hug, Miss Kate held onto me for a long time. To my shock, she whispered in my ear, "Thank you for taking such good care of my Patty."

My eyes flew to her face. Had she glimpsed Patty in one of my mirrors? (I had looked at each one, wondering if Lovey would appear, but I had seen no sign of her.) Or had Miss Kate somehow sensed her presence?

The others started to collect purses and notebooks and the treats Ellie brought them, so only Miss Kate could hear me say very softly, "You're very welcome. She has been such a comfort to me. Letting go while holding on is what we've both been doing, isn't it?"

She nodded and patted my arm. "Grief unites us, doesn't it?" she whispered. "You don't get used to it, but you just decide to move forward."

Tears misted my eyes when I nodded and promised, "I'll see you again soon. Very soon."

Anna took her hand and together they walked towards Jenny's car.

"What did she say?" Ellie asked. She must have guessed by my expression that something more meaningful than thanks had passed between us.

"I'll tell you later," I replied.

I knew that I would.

Eventually.

It wasn't until late that night that I could collect my thoughts and wonder about Miss Kate's extraordinary statement.

CHAPTER 8

Sunday

Karen and Jenny packed their rental car on Saturday evening with the treasures they had purchased at Marigold's and at other gift shops in the city. We all agreed to meet for breakfast at Annabelle's before our two new friends started their long drive back to Indiana.

Blueberry pancakes piled high with fresh whipped cream. Thick maple syrup served in antique gravy boats. Crispy home-cured bacon. Fresh fruit topped with homemade yoghurt. And a review of the amazing things that had happened during the course of the past week. Those were all on the menu.

The visit and new friendships and Miss Kate's words all seemed surreal to me in many ways, but it was Anna who summed up our week best when she said, "My dad will never believe all of this when he gets back from his golf trip tonight."

We laughed and agreed that he would indeed be surprised.

Eventually, reluctantly, after lots of hugs, laughter, and tears, Jenny and Karen accepted fresh hazelnut-flavored coffees in to-go cups, climbed into the rental car, pulled out of the parking lot at Annabelle's, and headed towards Interstate 16. I was sure their drive home to Indianapolis would go quickly, with all they had to discuss and recount.

As we watched the car disappear around the corner, Ellie said, "Everything appears to be the same, yet everything seems totally different now."

"This is going to take some time for me to let it all sink in," I added. But I wasn't ready to share with them a startling discovery I'd made that morning.

Lovey—Patty—had not appeared in my bedroom mirror, for the first time since I'd moved into the house fifteen years earlier. I visited every other mirror in the house, and then hurried over to Marigold's to check the mirrors there. She wasn't to be found.

In my mind, I tried to rationalize what her absence meant. After fifteen years, I learned that her name was Patty. I learned that she was a beloved ten-year-old daughter and friend who had suffered a tragic accident and premature death. I learned that she was still remembered, still loved, and still cherished. As I ran my hand across my empty bedroom mirror, I murmured, "You will always be Lovey to me. And, I will miss your sweet little smile."

But there was a part of me that was happy. I was convinced that her wandering spirit had learned she was still loved and remembered and cherished. Had she gone with her mother? I was guessing that she had. I sipped my coffee slowly as I considered my experience with a ghost. And then my mind snapped back to the present.

I saw Ellie hurry to the counter to speak with a customer. Anna returned to the table with a carafe of steaming coffee and I asked her about her classes.

" I've got some projects to finish up with my classes for this semester, " she told me. We chatted for a few moments before I stood, intending to head home. I was just about to ask about her boyfriend Grant when she interrupted.

"Do you know that man over there?" She nodded her head towards a good-looking dark-haired man seated across the room. He appeared to be in his early thirties, nicely dressed, and very nervous, judging by the way he was fiddling with his silverware and glancing around the cafe. When he noticed us looking at him, he quickly turned his head, but continued to arrange and rearrange the silverware.

"No, I don't think so. Why?" I asked

"Well, he keeps looking this way. I don't know him, either," she said, stealing another glance at him.

This time, when he noticed our attention, the man stood up and started walking towards us, his eyes fixed on me, his face quite pale.

"Hello," I said, when he was several feet from me. "Do I know you?" I felt unexpectedly wary and puzzled as I sat back down at the table.

"Not really," he said in a shaky voice. "But you know of me. I'm John Franklin, Jr. I'm the man responsible for all of your pain. I'm the man who killed your husband. I wanted—well, I really needed—to tell you how very sorry I am for your loss and my role in your loss."

"What!" I gasped. My voice must have been unusually loud, because heads turned all around Annabelle's crowded tables. I lowered my voice. "You're supposed to be in prison," I hissed, feeling frightened and furious at the same time. I could sense movement around me. Several people had gotten up and were coming towards me in support.

"I was just released. It's been ten years," he stammered.

But I couldn't really hear him because my ears were ringing. The room began to spin. I could see Anna open her mouth, calling for Ellie. I remember trying to keep my eyes open.

But everything went dark.

NOT THE END

Part Two

A
MESS
BECOMES
A
MESSAGE

CHAPTER 9

Sunday

Panic gripped me as I realized that John Franklin, Jr. was not only back in town, but he was back in my world. I opened my eyes to find that Ellie had draped cold kitchen towels around my neck. She was holding another to my forehead, and the icy water dripped down my nose and landed on my chin. Anna was holding tightly to my hand.

"Thanks, everyone, but Meg will be just fine," Ellie said, indicating that they could return to their tables. But still JFJ stood rooted to the floor in front of me. He kept apologizing, as if that would fix everything. Or anything.

"I think you've done enough damage for today," Ellie told him, not unkindly. "Perhaps it's best if you leave."

"I'm—I'm so sorry," he stammered.

Ellie nodded towards the door and he quickly left.

I had walked over to Annabelle's, but Ellie insisted on driving me home. I walked straight to the garden, to my Adirondack chair under the big oak tree, and collapsed. I needed to sit still and breathe, just breathe. And then I needed to talk to Jack, to feel his presence. I could hear and feel Ellie's comfort, but I was speechless and I felt as limp as a rag.

"Should I call your parents?" Ellie asked, watching me anxiously.

"No. Remember, they're on a three-month trip to the Mediterranean with friends," I said. "Right now they're probably on a boat somewhere. They can't really help, and I'm not going to ruin their long-awaited trip."

Ellie went into the kitchen and returned with a tall glass of ice water. "Is there anything I can do?" she asked anxiously.

"No. Thank you for what you're already done. I'll be fine. You're needed at Annabelle's," I told her, and watched her climb back into her SUV. We waved and she drove off.

Not many minutes later, I heard a car door slam and opened my eyes to see Paul Sanders, the senior partner of Jack's law firm—yes, I still considered it as Jack's firm—hurrying across the lawn to me. I saw the raw emotion on his face and heard it in his voice.

"Oh, Meghan, I'm so very sorry," he stammered, standing before me until I motioned him to a nearby chair. "I was supposed to be notified when Mr. Franklin was released. I had every intention of preparing you, so the shock wouldn't be so severe. It's bad enough that he was released a few months early, but to just show up at Annabelle's his first day out is unconscionable. I'm so very sorry."

I nodded as he squeezed my hand in sympathy. "But how did he know where I was?" I asked.

Although that really wasn't the most important question about the matter, it was to me at that moment.

"Apparently he came here, to your home, and was about to ring front doorbell when you walked around from the back. He followed you to Annabelle's," Mr. Sanders said. "I called his father—the judge—at his home since it is Sunday as soon as Ellie called me with the news. By that time, he was sitting there in his father's home office, talking everything over with the judge, apparently."

All I could think of at that moment was that I certainly would never answer the front door again if he had come to my home.

"But," I told Mr. Sanders, "I keep hearing the words, *I'm the man who killed your husband*, and I can't seem to unhear them."

I had known that one day soon John Franklin Jr. would be released from jail, but I hadn't known his sentence had been shortened for good behavior. After such a lovely week, full of new friends and fun times with Karen, Jenny, and Miss Kate, this was the last thing that I expected today.

"I'm appalled," Mr. Sanders said in his deep professional voice. "I'll get to the bottom of this, and I'll start the process of getting a restraining order if you need one. He told his father that he felt obliged to apologize in person to you, that it was one thing he thought of constantly over the last ten years."

We talked about Jack and the law firm and I calmed, but with suffocating sadness.

Mr. Sanders reached over and squeezed my hand again. We both had tears in our eyes. I know we both were thinking of Jack. Finally, I stood and asked if he wanted a cup of coffee or some sweet tea. He rose at the same time.

"No, my dear. Thank you, but I have a full Sunday ahead of me. I just wanted to be certain you were all right. I informed the judge in no uncertain terms that his son should stay far away from your home and Annabelle's, or I'd get a restraining order. He said he understood."

Mr. Sanders asked if there was anything he could do for me, and I thanked him, but said no. I walked him to his car, grateful for his support and the link he represented with Jack and his law firm.

"No worries," he said. "The moment Ellie called me, I was in the car."

I hadn't even thought to ask how he knew, but of course Ellie would have called him from the cafe. But who knew what JFJ had in mind after leaving his father's office?

Shortly after Mr. Sanders left, my cell rang. Ellie was calling to ask how I was doing.

I told her about Mr. Sander's visit and what he knew about JFJ's early release for good behavior. "I knew the day would come when he would get out of prison—and I knew it wasn't too far away. But it was a shock to see him face-to-face without warning," I told Ellie. I hesitated, then confessed, "I know that in my heart of hearts it was an accident and a senseless tragedy for all of us."

I didn't have to tell Ellie what I was thinking: a supposedly brilliant young man from a stellar family had spent nearly ten years behind bars because he made a stupid, tragic decision. But he would one day return to his family. My brilliant young husband had paid for that young man's stupid, tragic decision with his life—and he wouldn't be returning to his family. Ever.

"I have such a capable staff that I can leave Annabelle's to them today," Ellie said. "I'm coming over."

She arrived with two plates piled high with our favorite salad and a bag holding slices of french bread. She ate ravenously and I tried to eat while we sat together in the garden talking about everything but the topic uppermost in my mind.

An hour later, I insisted that Ellie should return to her bustling café. She refused at first, until I convinced her that I was okay. The shock had worn off for both of us, but we are friendship sisters, and as close as any biological sisters, and we feel each other's pain.

Finally, Ellie was convinced. As we stood, we hugged. "Another chapter in our lives is unfolding," she whispered. "I'm here for you, for anything you need. But you know that."

I nodded, and I tried to keep the tremor out of my voice when I said, with a conviction I didn't feel, "Surely he won't try to contact me again or show up at Annabelle's."

"He wouldn't dare! I'll whack him with my rolling pin," Ellie said, grinning. But she hugged me again.

After Ellie left, I sighed and walked to Marigold's with Lucy. "Work, Lucy. That's what I need. Let's find something fun to do." I glanced around my shop and saw the last remaining box I had purchased at the estate sale. "Let's hope we can find a wonderful surprise here," I muttered, pulling off the first layer of tissue paper.

"Wow! I didn't have to look very hard," I told Lucy, who was sunning herself in a patch of sunlight on a cushion at my feet. To my delight, I unwrapped several cut glass bowls that were just stunning. They would be even more beautiful once I washed them from years of non-use.

CHAPTER 10

Monday

The sun came up long after I was already awake. I had dreamed all night of Jack and the courtroom scene when I first saw John Franklin Jr. Over and over again I saw JFJ's eyes staring into my face, and every time, I awoke and sat upright in bed, startled yet again. "I'm a survivor. I'm a survivor. I've moved on," I reminded myself. "That accident will not define me."

However, sometimes those reminders are easier said than done.

I got out of bed and moved in the direction of the shower, hoping to clear my head. I glanced in the mirror, but my sweet Lovey was not there smiling back at me.

The blank mirror made me feel both happy and lonely. I had been greeted by her bright, smiling face every day for the past fifteen years—until this week. "But, of course she needs to find her peace," I reminded myself, speaking out loud. "And I truly believe that has now happened." Yet again, I marveled at the chance acquaintance with Jenny that led to a friendship with her mother, Karen. And how our friendship with Karen led us to Miss Kate and the story of a very special and tragic family who once lived in my home. What a gift these new friends had become in such a very short time.

As I toweled my hair dry, I glanced out the window and saw the sun shining. Today was living up to the weatherman's prediction: sunny, beautiful weather. Reaching 68 degrees by late afternoon, according to the news. "Not too hot and not too cool, Lucy," I told my sleepy cat as she climbed stiff-legged from her cushion. "It's a perfect March day."

I dressed in a pair of khaki capris and a soft red spring sweater with three-quarter sleeves. After putting on my makeup and some cute gold earrings, I fastened my cuff bracelet to my wrist. "Well, today will be a better day," I promised myself as we walked to the kitchen. I opened the kitchen door so I could hear the birds sing as I drank my first cup of coffee and painted my nails a bright read, the exact shade of the roses blooming beside my window. And still, it wasn't quite seven o'clock in the morning.

"Well, let's get an early start to our day," I announced. I decided to snip some apple mint from my garden and then walk over to Annabelle's for breakfast. I wanted to get back on track today, returning to the happy feelings that had filled the past week. I knew I couldn't revert back to the shattered pieces—and the shattered woman—of the past. I thought I might also need to reassure Anna that I was, truly, fine. I knew that Jack's accident had forced that young girl to deal with too much pain, confusion, and drama.

I was thinking about my first appointment of the day as I headed to breakfast. After I had discussed with a group of realtors my ideas about staging houses to appear at their very best before they went on the market, they asked to hear more of my ideas, see some examples, and listen to testimonials about the effectiveness of staging houses to expedite sales.

Just as I was about to reach for Annabelle's door, Anna came bouncing out, looking adorable in white skinny jeans and a watermelon colored pink tee-shirt.

"Hi, honey," I said, smiling at her joyful face. "I came to see you before you go to class."

"How are you, Meg?" she asked, looking at me anxiously.

I gave her a big smile. "I'm perfectly fine, and I don't want you to worry. There's absolutely nothing to worry about." Then I grinned at her. "Can I buy you a muffin? I happen to know a place where the muffins are absolutely delicious."

"Ha-ha!" She returned my grin. "Besides the fact that I made one batch of those muffins, you know that you and I are on the 'free list' with Mom." Then the smile faded, and Anna shook her head. "He looked like a nice guy, Meg. I was so shocked when he said who he was—but not as shocked as you were." She looked thoughtful. "I always imagined what he would look like—and I imagined a monster, not someone who looks like he stepped out of the pages of a magazine."

"I know, honey, I haven't seen him in ten years, so of course he has aged, but he was the last person I expected yesterday." I sighed and forced myself to smile. "But other than that one glitch in our week, we had an amazing time with our new friends, didn't we? So let's just hang on to that thought."

Anna smiled and said how much she liked Miss Kate, and that she planned to see her again soon. "And Jenny will be returning with her writing friends, so we didn't really say goodbye yesterday," I added.

Anna reached for Annabelle's door latch, bowed low, and waved me in. "I'm starving! Let's eat together before I go to class. I was planning on spending time in the library first, but I'm too hungry for a mere muffin. I think we should order the works. "

I didn't really have much appetite, but I knew Anna continued to watch me closely, so we both ordered steel-cut oatmeal with fresh raspberries and cream as well as a muffin. Ellie came over to hug me. No words needed.

Anna was just finishing up when Annabelle's door opened again, and Grant entered. "Here is your very handsome boyfriend," I announced, smiling at the husky blond football player who had become as dear to me as he is to Anna's parents.

Anna smiled. "I texted him to pick me up here." They ordered coffees to go. I watched them leave the café hand-in-hand. I couldn't help but sigh a little at the adoring looks they gave each other. Their future seemed as full of love and promise as Jack's and mine had once looked.

When Ellie had a moment to drop into Anna's vacated chair with a cup of tea in her hand, I passed her the bouquet of apple mint, still damp with dew. "Thanks for this," Ellie said. "The first fifty or so tea customers will love this extra treat."

"My pleasure," I said. "The chocolate and pineapple mint will be ready to snip soon. I haven't decided which I enjoy the most."

"Sounds yummy." Ellie spread raspberry jam on her scone. "So what's on your agenda today?"

I told her about the appointment with the realtors and two other appointments that would take place during store hours. She was about to ask another question when a group arrived for their breakfast meeting, so she winked at me, rose, and hurried to greet them.

I walked directly to Marigold's. At ten o'clock promptly, the three realtors arrived, and I invited them to sit at the farm table, nibble on strawberry almond breakfast bars, and sip sweet tea as we looked at photographs of the interiors of homes they had listed. I discussed the ways staging these homes would help increase traffic and promote faster sales.

"People always enjoy getting new ideas," I explained. "Sometimes someone visits because they want ideas for expanding living space and/or redecorating their own homes. Some are considering buying another home but they need to freshen up their home to make it marketable. The theory is that you decorate a home to live in it but you stage it to sell it. The difference is that when a home is staged, potential buyers don't have to imagine what a room would look like without toys on the floor and mismatched furniture throughout the place. It is recommended that sellers remove as many personal items as possible so a potential buyer can see themselves in the space not the seller."

I handed each of them a fact sheet about staging, and reiterated what the facts stated: "Staged houses sell for between six and seventeen percent more than non-staged houses—and twice as fast." I gave them several references from previous staging projects.

"Will you use some of the items from your shop when you stage a house?" one realtor asked as the group slowly toured my shop. "I love everything in your inventory—it's perfect for that 'sophisticated country atmosphere' you mentioned," she added.

"Remember, ladies," I said, "you DECORATE to live in your home, as I gestured around the shop but you STAGE to sell."

" However, if the seller has moved and the home is empty then I will gladly take a few important pieces to your listings to add warmth and give the potential buyer ideas." I stated.

And then they saw the Friendship Board. They read each story aloud, taking turns to exclaim over the notes, review the classes scheduled, and the decorating notes & quotes.

At the end of the hour, I agreed to come speak at their company's weekly meeting, to open the discussion for other realtors and to share more statistics and ideas about staging. Before they left, I signed contracts with the three realtors for ten of their listings that needed staging. After I waved goodbye to them, I returned to the shop feeling more excited than I had felt in months. I looked forward to helping my business continue to expand in new and unexpected directions.

I checked my watch and realized that I would be just on time for my next appointment. Grabbing a bottled water, I headed to my white Tahoe, which, fortunately, was already loaded with my bag, which overflowed with measuring tapes, paint chips, fabric swatches, and photographs of room designs.

My first stop was to meet a new customer who had bought a stately 19th-century row house in the oldest part of town. She was interested in renovating and redecorating her kitchen—which is one of my favorite projects. "You will love it when we're done," I promised her.

On my second appointment, I met a new bride whose bridesmaids had given her a gift certificate to transform her bland beige apartment into a warm welcoming first home. (The previous year I had begun offering gift certificates as shower or wedding presents. They are truly appreciated—and no one ever asks to return them.)

"I need to make this small space home for a year, while my husband finishes graduate school," the bride said. I assured her that we could pull it all together.

As I measured the living space, we discussed her color preferences and current trends in paint and wallpapers. I suggested ideas for possible dual-use areas. She had a second bedroom, which she needed for her many out-of-town guests, but she also needed a home office.

"I love finding creative ways to decorate and live with an open floor plan," I told her. "It can be a challenge when you have a combination kitchen, living room, and dining area separated only by a half wall. I also noted the lovely family pieces that had been given to her and a pile of gifts yet to be stored away. "I'll work on floor plans and ideas for additional storage," I promised.

I scheduled a return visit in a few days, when I would bring my ideas. I urged her to get approval from her landlord regarding painting the walls.

When I headed home to grab a quick lunch, my mind was spinning with ideas from all three morning appointments. I was anxious to start sketching and inventorying. I quickly made a turkey, brie cheese, and tomato sandwich, spreading the sourdough bread with mayo mixed with fresh basil from my garden. After I filled a glass with ice cubes and peach tea, I put my lunch on a tray. On my way to Marigold's, I stopped for a handful of cosmos to fill the vase on the shop counter. After unlocking my shop and flipping the sign to "open," Lucy walked slowly to her cushion near the window and lay down to sleep in the sun.

I wandered around the big, cheerful space, munching on my sandwich and smiling to myself. "This shop makes me so happy!" I said out loud, smiling at Lucy when she lifted her head at the sound of my voice.

I had hung three panels of darling shower curtains on a wooden dowel and I studied their colors, admiring these one-of-a-kind curtains that I had purchased from a very talented lady by the name of Linda Unger. She buys quilt tops, those that are pieced together but not finished, and adds a colorful print backing and twelve button holes across the top. They give a beautiful and elegant tone to a bathroom, yet they have a vintage look that would complement any cottage or farmhouse-style decor. She had recently brought me an assortment in various contemporary color combinations and quilt patterns. She also delivered six square quilted pillows made from vintage floral fabrics. As I studied them, I knew they would fly out the door once the right customers saw them. I reminded myself to order more soon. Our local newspaper had written a design feature about Linda's work. With the word out, customers would come looking for them. Fortunately, the article mentioned my shop as one source.

Just then, when I was lost in my thoughts, I heard voices from my porch. Four ladies entered the shop talking all at once, even finishing each other's sentences. "Hello," they all chimed. "We're college friends enjoying an antiquing road trip together. We just stopped for a late lunch—which was out of this world—and Annabelle's sent us here!"

I welcomed them and had the best time listening to their stories about their days as sorority roommates many years ago as they browsed through the shop. "What do you collect?" and "What would you like to start collecting?" are two questions that trigger great conversations in Marigold's. An hour later, after several trips to their car with arms loaded with packages, they said goodbye. "We're heading for a spa appointment," one shopper—the last to leave the shop—told me.

The rest of the afternoon was equally busy. I worked on design ideas and restocked all the shelves after the recent spending spree. All three shower curtains had disappeared. I placed a call to Linda.

I had finished my day's work and was preparing to close the shop when I saw a black sports car pull to the curb. DOC climbed out, and I walked onto the porch to greet him. I was pleased, but puzzled, to see him return to Marigold's.

"Hi, DOC," I said, smiling into his smiling eyes. "Don't tell me you need more platters!"

"No," he grinned. "I'm off the hook for gifts—at least for the moment—but I do need to talk to you." He looked at the empty rockers on the porch and the key in my hand. "Is this a bad time?" he asked.

"Not at all! I was just closing for the day," I said. "Let me flip the sign and we can sit here on the porch or in the garden and talk."

I gestured for him to join me on the path that wound past flowering trees and blooming azaleas and eventually we reached a pair of Adirondack chairs surrounded by spring flowers. "Please sit and relax," I invited. "I imagine you're exhausted after your day." He nodded and I thought of his mother, who is one of my best customers. "Is your mom doing okay?" I inquired.

"Oh, yes. She's doing great," he said. "This isn't about her."

When I raised my eyebrows, he continued. "I need to tell you that I recognized you when I was here the last time. For the ironstone platter, that is. I couldn't place you at first, but then the memory came slowly back to me."

Taking on a more clinical tone, he explained, "You got so pale when I said that I worked in the ER that I figured something had happened there. But eventually I remembered your face and the way you fix your hair. I remembered you and the horrible day when your husband was killed. I didn't want you to think that I knew who you were and failed to offer my condolences again."

I was quiet a minute, remembering the scene in the ER when I arrived. I admitted, "I was like you. I didn't recognize you at first because that day is a blur, but when you mentioned the ER at Memorial Hospital and I saw you looking at me as if you were trying to place me, the details started to come back. There are days when ten years feels like ten minutes, when I think of my husband."

I told him how coincidental it was that he came by. Then I described the scene in Annabelle's the previous morning. "The driver, John Franklin Jr, had just been released from prison, and he decided to let me know in person," I said, feeling a little breathless.

I could see that he had no idea what to say to that other than, "I'm so sorry," so I quickly changed the subject. We chatted about my garden, his sister's wedding, and the weather. Eventually he said he was working the night shift and needed to leave. "When I passed Marigold's, stopping had been an impulse," he said. "But I'm very glad to see you again, Meg." He held out his hand and took mine.

I thanked him for coming to see me and for telling me that he had been with Jack in the hospital. "That's a link that I appreciate even after all of these years," I told him. "I knew that Jack had received the best care, but now I knew who had actually been part of the trauma team.

He nodded and began walking to his car. I watched him go, intending to pick some flowers for my kitchen table, when he turned and retraced his steps. "Would you consider having coffee with me some morning?" he asked in a rush. "I know a great café called Annabelle's, just a couple blocks over."

I laughed. "Yes, I know all about Annabelle's. My very best friend owns it." Then the smile faded from my face. "But I'll probably decline meeting you—with thanks for your kind offer," I said.

"I understand," he said, squeezing my hand. "But maybe I'll see you there one morning and let you know how your platter is doing," he added with a charming smile.

I laughed. "Please do!" I said. And, I added, "Thank you for stopping by today, DOC. And thank you for caring."

I turned toward my kitchen door, temporarily forgetting my plans to pick a bouquet. I had been starving ten minutes earlier, but now I found I wasn't really very hungry. I grabbed an apple and walked out to my chair by the oak tree. My mind was whirling full speed.

"Oh, Jack." I sighed. "What a day! I need you to know that DOC just told me what you must already know: the doctors did everything they could for you on that last day, but your injuries were too severe."

Of course, I already knew that, but the fact that this particular doctor had been right there fighting for Jack somehow comforted me. I continued the conversation, "DOC also asked me to meet him for coffee, but I declined. It was only coffee, but, Jack, I only have room in my heart for one man. You."

I put my hand up to my head to shade my eyes. "This has certainly been an emotional couple of days," I murmured. I finished talking to myself, somehow feeling better. It's why I call it a healing garden.

CHAPTER 11

Tuesday

I was just walking across the garden to open Marigold's when I saw Mr. Sanders' navy blue Lexus park in front of my house. Immediately my heart started fluttering.

"Hello, Mr. Sanders." I hoped my voice sounded relaxed and friendly when I found him walking through the garden in my direction, but when I saw his face, I added quickly, "I'm doing okay. Sunday was traumatic, but it's over."

At that moment, I saw Ellie turn the corner of my garden and walk up to us with coffees and a bag of something sweet-smelling. That's when I began to realize this was a planned meeting.

"What's going on?" I asked, glancing from one to the other.

"I tried to call you a few minutes ago," Ellie said, "to tell you that Mr. Sanders had dropped by Annabelle's, hoping to see you, and that he was on his way. But you didn't answer. I just hurried over, in case you didn't want to be alone."

She hugged me and whispered in my ear, "I don't have a clue what he wants, but he looked serious when he asked about you."

"Sorry!" I said. "I must have left my cellphone on the kitchen island. Please, sit, both of you. I'll just run in and get it, in case anyone else needs me." I dashed into the house as they settled around the garden table, wishing I could stay there and not hear whatever Mr. Sanders had come to tell me.

"I'm sorry to stop in unannounced," Mr. Sanders began.

"What's wrong?" I felt breathless when I spoke.

"I spoke to Mr. Franklin and his father yesterday at length," he said.

"Oh?" That was all I could think to say, but my stomach seemed full of tiny fluttering birds.

"They asked to meet me at my office this morning," he said. When he saw the look on my face, he quickly added, "Once again, they both apologized for Mr. Franklin's unexpected appearance at Annabelle's on Sunday."

I wondered where this was going. Mr. Sanders wrinkled his brow and pressed his fingers together, as I had seen him do in the courtroom on more than one occasion. "Meg," he said, "He wants to meet with you again, this time a proper, pre-arranged meeting."

He must have sensed I was going to decline because he said, "Mr. Franklin wants to tell you how he plans to make amends. He has spent the last ten years formulating a plan to help others, but he wants your blessing. He has considered his career plans carefully."

"I have absolutely no interest in his career plans, as long as he stays away from alcohol," I said heatedly.

Mr. Sanders sounded like my father when he said, "Meg, he needs you to hear his message. Most of all, he says, he needs your forgiveness."

"Forgive him for killing my husband? I don't think so!" When I realized I must sound hysterical, I lowered my voice.

"Well, I've told him that I'm not sure whether any of what he wants is possible, but I told him that I, as your friend and your attorney, would discuss his request with you." He finished with a sigh.

"I don't want to talk to him—ever! And I don't care what he does with his career. I find some satisfaction in the fact that his dream of becoming a lawyer won't be realized, since none of Jack's dreams were realized." Once again I realized I was shouting. I lowered my voice.

"Well, there is more that you need to know," Mr. Sanders said, ignoring my raised voice. "I've told him, as well as his father, that you and Ellie are very active with the local chapter of Mothers Against Drunk Driving, that you have tried to help others who find themselves in your circumstances, not just mothers, and that you are committed to lobbying for new legislation about drunk driving. I also told them that you have been trying to move forward with your life, not dwell on the past any more than you have to."

"And?" I asked. I put my hands up to my cheeks, which felt like marble.

"Meg, this is painful for all of us. You know that I thought of Jack like a son," Mr. Sanders said, reaching for my hand.

"I know."

"On the other hand," he continued, "The lives of all members of the Franklin family have also been forever changed too. They are trying to reach out to you and others to let you know that you're not alone, that they will do everything in their power to change the course of the future."

When I looked skeptical, Mr. Sanders said, "John Franklin Jr has agreed never to approach you if you decline his offer of a meeting. This is totally your choice, Meg. I'll support your decision either way." He wiped his hand over his forehead. I noticed that Mr. Sanders seemed to have aged since Sunday.

I could feel Ellie's hand squeeze my shoulder. I glanced at her and discovered that she had tears running down her cheeks, just as I did.

"This is beyond bold on his part," I started to say. "But," I added slowly, "I'll think about it. I know I need to move forward. I can't stand the idea of going through any more pain or unpleasantness over all of this again, but maybe—maybe—I'll listen to his story. It's important to me to learn if he truly is sorry."

"That's all I can ask for," Mr. Sanders said.

"I'll let you know soon, Mr. Sanders."

He stood up and, to my surprise, kissed me on the forehead. "Take good care of yourself, my dear." I watched him walk to his car in silence.

Ellie and I sat without speaking, staring into the distance for a few minutes, shaking our heads in disbelief.

I was grateful when she changed the subject, rather than dwelling on it or offering advice. "Where are those cute quilt shower curtains you told me about?" she asked in a cheerful voice.

"Gone," I said smiling for the first time all morning. "Now, my dear friend, go back to Annabelle's." I stood and grabbed my cell phone and shop keys. "I'm good—really. I have a group coming soon for a one of my favorite classes, 'The Collected Cottage.' We'll talk about paints, beautiful old woods, wire planters, wicker baskets, Depression glass, and—of course—white ironstone dishes. All my favorite things. That will make me happy."

"I remembered," she said. "And you have chocolate pecan brownies in a baker box inside this bag. Have fun and we'll talk about Mr. Sanders' news later."

"Later," I promised.

"Hey," I called out to her as she started to leave, "remind me to tell you about a doctor named DOC who was with Jack when he died in the ER. I met him when he came to buy an ironstone platter."

"That sounds interesting. Tell me more!"

"Of course I will but too little time right now. But add it to the list and I'll catch up with you later. Have a good day," I called to her. "And, thanks for not forgetting the brownies in all of the confusion this morning. Love you, Ellie!"

I reached Marigold's just minutes ahead of my first customers. I flipped the sign to "open," and started my class immediately.

The day seemed to fly by—and I was grateful. I didn't have time to think about anything but the business. Just as I reached to switch off the shop lights, a well-dressed middle-aged lady poked her head into the shop. Smiling, she introduced herself as Carla

Simon. When I saw a briefcase in her hand, my first thought was that she had something to do with John Franklin Jr.

"Hello." I greeted her cautiously. "I'm Meg, the owner of Marigold's. You look like you're on a mission, so how may I help you?"

She introduced herself as a reporter for our local newspaper. "I've heard all about your flourishing business, and I wondered if you would consider allowing me to interview you for a feature article about Marigold's. Would you mind?"

Relief flooded me as I realized the visit was not about JFJ.

"I'd be flattered," I told her. "Please come in, sit down, and tell me more about your assignment."

"As you must know, the Sunday addition always features a Home and Garden section, and I thought that I could feature Marigold's. I've been assigned to write a cover-page feature on decorating trends, with a sidebar on advice from a decorator. I've asked around, and your name keeps coming up as a great source."

"That's great!" I said. "When do you want to begin? Now?"

"No, I know this is the end of your day," she said. We set up an appointment, and she asked, "Do you mind if I take some pictures?"

"Not at all." I marveled at the upturn to my day.

Before leaving, the reporter wandered around the shop, ending her tour at the Friendship Board. "Can you tell me about this?" she asked.

"Of course—and so much more."

Later, I sat in my kitchen with one ear on the news, eating a bowl of homemade potato soup with garden herbs. Lucy rubbed against my ankle, and I looked down at her and reminded her, "Life is certainly full of surprises, and I'm grateful that today ended with such a nice surprise."

I pulled out one of Jack's yellow legal pads and started jotting down notes about the business and ideas for the interview, knowing it would not only be fun, but it might mean additional business for my shop. I listed the people I wanted to mention: Ellie, of course, who supplied my endless variety of cookies. Linda and her quilted accessories. And Anna, who had just delivered some chalk painted pieces with a waxed finish to my shop inventory.

The thought of Anna and her art projects made me smile. Months ago she designed and painted garden sticks a pale green with the words Parsley, Mint, Basil, Thyme, Dill, Rosemary and Sage written in bold print. The weatherproof signs had quickly become favorites with customers who gardened. She had recently spoken to me about bringing in a few small pieces of painted and decorated furniture—benches, shelves, and small straight chairs.

The list of my creative suppliers continued to grow as I made notes.

CHAPTER 12

Wednesday

The night was long but I finally dosed off sometime after three am, tucked into my bed with soft linens and my antique quilt. I needed comfort, and I found it as soon as I woke up, by looking at the photographs on my cherry dresser. Was I looking for an answer to Mr. Sanders' proposal? Or was I just saying good morning to Jack? I wasn't really sure, but I got up feeling calmer. By the time I was ready for the day, however, my mind was racing.

Deep in thought, I sat in my breakfast nook for a very long time, eating cheesy scrambled eggs with fresh herbs from my garden. I needed to sort through my thoughts, so I walked over to the kitchen desk for another of Jack's yellow legal pads and a pen. I smiled to myself as I remembered that Jack had found me this big boxy oak teachers desk at our favorite antique store. He had spent long hours during the winter of our first married year refinishing it for my first office. After his death, when I closed my office and moved the desk home, it fit into this corner of my kitchen perfectly.

But, back to work. I listed questions that started and ended with Jack. Did I really need to talk with

JFJ? Could a meeting help me in any way? Would a meeting hurt me? Was he really sorry or just following his father's request for proper behavior? Did he really plan to make amends, not just to me, but to other families somehow? Did he really have a career plan based around this tragedy? Would listening to him just open up old wounds again for all of us? What good would come of it? On the other hand, could this be the opportunity for the final piece of me to heal? What would Jack want me to do? I took my list with me as Lucy and I passed through the garden to Marigold's.

The day was full of phone calls with requests to schedule appointments. After scanning the newspaper, I added a couple of upcoming estate sales to my calendar, planning to attend. I called Linda to inquire about the delivery of more shower curtain quilts and learned that she had other products, among them memo boards backed with colorful quilt pieces. "Hopefully, I'll deliver them in the next few days," she told me.

Anna arrived in the late afternoon and worked on our blog about the Friendship Board. I had emails from several friends looking for specific pieces of glassware, and one request for Sweetgrass Baskets typically made in Charleston for her collection. Another writer had visited my shop while on vacation; her finds at Marigold's had inspired her California friends to follow my postings.

The requests were numerous, and tracking down all the items would give me some interesting challenges to enjoy. I also had several appointments for "skype decorating" after my first project proved to be a success. I found it was fun to decorate a house cross country, without leaving home. "I think we've found a new version of the old pen pal theme," I told my satisfied customer.

But Anna was less concerned about my business progress than the list laying on my counter. After a couple of minutes she asked quietly, "What do you plan to do, Meg?"

I sighed and dropped into a chair at the farm table. "I really don't know, Anna," I told her. "I'm reviewing all the points that you see there, thinking over the answers to all those questions—and, as you can see, there are a lot of them. Then I'll try to make the best decision. I don't want you to worry about any of this," I added, crossing the room to hug her.

"I'm not worried," she said. "But do you want my thoughts?"

"Of course."

"Well," she said slowly, "My Jack said to tell you to listen to JFJ, make no comment—after all, you don't owe him any response—and then let it all go and move on. My Jack said he wants you to live your life happily."

"Really?" I gasped.

And so I followed Anna's advice. I called Mr. Sanders and agreed to a meeting, but with very specific terms. It would be held at Annabelle's—for several reasons. First, I feel safe there, and I don't want him in my home or Marigold's. Secondly, because Annabelle's is the location of the monthly MADD meeting. I wanted him to know the stories woven into the fabric of this organization, starting with the day in 1980, when Candy Lightner lost her thirteen-year-old daughter because of a drunk driver. She made it her mission to establish an organization aptly named MADD, to help prevent that tragedy happening for others.

I decided that I needed John Franklin Jr to know that victims find recovery by helping others. Mentally, I reviewed the list of our chapter members: parents and friends of seriously injured children and survivors of tragedies where someone they loved had been killed. JFJ didn't just take my husband's life. He robbed me of the chance to have children of my own. He robbed our friends. He robbed the community and Jack's firm.

After dinner, I called Mr. Sanders and told him that I would agree to meet JFJ on Friday at seven o'clock at night, it could be scheduled at Annabelle's. He asked me why I decided to accept. I outlined the reasons. "I'm not sure that I can ever forgive him, but I can accept that he is trying to make amends," I told Mr. Sanders. "He appears to be trying to turn a mess into a message, and I hope that will prevent others from making his mistake."

CHAPTER 13

Thursday

Having the decision-making behind me started the day well. I was eating a bowl of fresh fruit and a thick slice of cinnamon toast at Annabelle's while reading the local paper when DOC arrived. I noticed that he looked exhausted.

"Hi," he said. He seemed hesitant to approach my table until I beckoned him over.

"Good morning." I smiled. "Are you coming or going? You look really tired."

He stifled a yawn and nodded. "I just finished a twelve-hour shift, and I'm starving. I knew this would be the place to find great food in a hurry before going home to crash." He confessed, "I'm not much of a cook."

When I introduced Ellie, she shook his hand and told him. "I've seen you here a few times, but you always seem to get away before I can properly meet you. Let me get a server to take your order quickly."

"Ellie likes to know all of her customers, so I'm surprised you haven't met," I said. It also explained to me how she didn't recognize the name DOC when I mentioned the two visits and conversations I'd had with the handsome doctor.

"Do you mind if I sit here? Or would you rather I move to another table?" he asked. "I don't want to make you feel uncomfortable."

"Please, sit," I said, pointing to the chair Ellie had just vacated. We chatted about the great food, the spring weather, his mother, everything but the ER. By the time his food arrived, I felt as if he were a long-lost friend. Hesitating just a moment, I told him about the latest JFJ request for a meeting.

He didn't answer right away, but when he did, I appreciated his thoughtful response. "I'm not sure what to say to that, except that you're an exceptional person moving through unbelievably difficult times," he said. Then he asked with a concerned look in his eyes, "Can I help you in any way?"

"Thank you, but I think this is my journey," I said. "I'm trying to close this ten-year-long chapter of my life and create a new normal for the rest of my life." I paused, then spoke a sudden realization. "I was doing so well until he showed up here last Sunday. Now, I'm a little off balance, but determined to move on. That's a new resolution for me."

"Good for you!" he said, encouragingly. He seemed to have forgotten his hunger and his breakfast as we talked. At last we both finished eating and started for the door.

"Good luck Friday evening," he said, adding, "and I really hope that I run into you again for breakfast."

"Thanks so much. Me, too," I replied. I meant that for both comments.

The day was filled with interesting customers and fun conversations. My class about creating curb appeal for homes and businesses went very well. By seven o'clock, the farm table was set and ready for the monthly meeting of my book club. We gather the third Thursday of every month, and we eat our way through a discussion of the latest book selection. This night was our semi-annual meeting, where we celebrate all of our members' birthdays, if they fall within the upcoming six months. We also select the books to read for the next six months.

Ellie had told me she was bringing Hummingbird Cake, a yummy combination of bananas, pineapple and pecans added to a cinnamon flavored cake batter . The layers and top would be a thick cream cheese icing. And, of course I had plenty of cold sweet tea, or *Wine of the South* as it is known. We would add one candle for each of the birthday celebrants because we consider us all number one. Despite meeting only twelve times a year, we are close friends and we all support each other. This fun group of eight "girls" represent a huge range of ages, various backgrounds, and all types of careers. What we all have in common is our love of reading.

My farm table was chosen as our permanent location right after Marigold's opened, and my job was to provide drinks and maintain the list of the books we've read and plan to read.

CHAPTER 14

Friday

My friend Melissa Campbell was the first friend I saw this morning. She does fabulous upholstery work. She's quick, and she has an eye for fabric and design. Today she brought me back a chaise that I bought at an estate sale two months earlier.

"It has great lines," she said as I exclaimed over the transformation. "It was covered in one nasty faded print," she agreed.

"Melissa, this new cream-colored corduroy textile is stunning!" I marveled. "I can't believe it's the same chaise—but I trusted you to know what would work." As I walked around the furniture to admire it from all angles, I told her, "This will be all the rage with my customers. It can be placed in a living room, family room, bedroom, or sunroom because that textile is so versatile. Or," I added, looking up at her with my confession, "it just may find its way up the gravel path to my living room."

Melissa laughed. "I wouldn't have minded adding this to my décor, either. It turned out so well that I'm not sure I can let go of it. But this isn't all I brought you, Meg."

Next we carried in a pair of wingback chairs. These, too, looked brand new and dramatically different from their original faded, outdated print. Melissa had chosen navy-and-white ticking, which made them look clean, modern, and perfect for an urban cottage look.

"And lastly, take a look at this big square ottoman whose leather was shredded," she said, pointing to what was coming up the porch stairs. She had covered the ottoman in black-and-white cowhide. I couldn't stop staring at it. "You're so talented." I said. My friend laughed, hugged me and hurried down the porch steps. "I've got a busy morning," she said, waving.

As I stood pondering the chaise and my living room decor, I received a text from Jenny, asking, "Can Mom and I skype with you and Ellie??? We have great ideas to discuss about return in late April!"

I immediately responded: "Of course. Give me some times when you're free and I'll check with Ellie. We can't wait to see you again!"

Originally, this was supposed to be my afternoon off, but I knew that with the meeting at 6:30, I needed to stay busy. So I changed into gardening clothes, gathered a rake, hoe, clippers, and attacked the garden. A couple hours later, I had pulled weeds, filled the bird feeders, pruned rosebushes, moved a couple of urns, and added annuals to my flower beds. Gardening always gives me peace when I need it most. After making a salad for lunch, I brought it under the oak tree and thought about all that could happen tonight—and what I wished would happen. Just as I was about to head into the house to shower and dress for the meeting, I heard Jack's voice in my ear.

"Love you, love of my life. You'll be fine—better than fine. It is time now to move on with your life."

I put my hand over my heart and blew a kiss to the skies before I began the walk to Annabelle's in the early evening fading sunlight. The café is only a block away from my home, but on this night, it seemed miles away.

Jack's best friend Mark, Ellie's husband, met me at the café door. He greeted me with a hug and a smile, saying, "I know this is hard for you, Meg, but we here for you." Anna and Ellie came from the kitchen, carrying a pitcher of sweet tea, a carafe of coffee, and a platter of peanut butter cookies.

"I doubt that anyone will be able to eat a thing, but it's the thought that counts," she said, more to herself than me. I could tell she was nervous—more nervous than I had seen her in a very long time.

Promptly at 6:30, Mr. Sanders, Judge John Franklin, and John Franklin Jr arrived. I was struck by how much the son looked like the father, and how careworn and uncomfortable they both appeared to be. Introductions were made by Mr. Sanders. The judge clasped my hand firmly and looked into my eyes without saying a word. Then John Franklin, Jr. squared his shoulders and walked up to me. Standing alone and vulnerable, he spoke directly to me.

"I will never forgive myself for what I did to you, your family, your friends, and to my own family," he said. "So I know I can't expect you to forgive me. However, if I may, I'd like to tell you that I am trying to make amends."

He told me that he had completed a law degree while he was in prison. "But, of course I can never sit for the bar exam," he added, and I could see the tears in his eyes. "I will never become a trial lawyer as I had planned, but I can become much more."

John Franklin, Jr had a tragic look on his face that might have mirrored the look on my own face when he took a deep breath and proceeded, "I plan to utilize my educational and personal experience to help educate teens, college students, young adults, and yes, even older adults, about the tragic consequences of alcohol. I hope to reach everyone who thinks that this could never happen to them."

He told me that he had already done extensive research about alcoholism and the life-changing and life-threatening statistics involved in drunk driving accidents. "I'll teach and consult because I can do that in a private practice," he said. "I plan to work with Mothers Against Drunk Driving—I've already reached out to their national organization—and other groups. Mrs. Kingston, I promise I will be a tireless volunteer in the cause, both locally and nationally. I plan to make a difference in the only way possible now."

I saw a proud expression cross the judge's face as his son continued speaking. "I will use myself as an example of changing behaviors and direction." John Franklin Jr. glanced down at his tightly clenched hands. I knew he was trying to keep them from shaking—and perhaps keep himself from crying. "I wasn't a bad person," he said in a choked voice. "But I did a bad thing, and so many people have suffered because of it."

He explained that while he was in prison, he had read news articles announcing the start of a new MADD chapter here, and he had seen my name listed as a founder, along with Ellie's name and the location at Annabelle's. "I know that you help fund professional counseling when victims can't afford it," he said. "And I read that your own story of survival is shared to give hope to others. You are a remarkable woman. I've waited ten years to offer my sincere apology. Again I'm sorry for barging in on you on Sunday. It just seemed that I couldn't get to you fast enough to offer my apology. I've kept it inside me for ten long years in prison."

I was struggling to control my own tears, and I thought he had finished speaking when John Franklin Jr. added, "I've also put my family—especially my father, who is a judge in this city—in an incredibly difficult position. I will devote myself to my new career on behalf of your husband, an outstanding lawyer who didn't get to pursue his career long enough." After he finished speaking, he took a long, shaky breath.

I really could not say a thing for a few minutes. Then I looked at him and wiped the tears from my eyes.

"Ten years ago, my heart and my life were shattered. Tonight, well tonight, maybe it has started to heal. Thank you for your words. I do believe you." I reached out to shake his hand. "I learned a long time ago that when people talk about the pain in their lives—whatever it might be—then they start to heal. For all of us here, the 'it' is when an inebriated person gets behind the wheel and drives onto the road, jeopardizing the lives of so many innocent people." I tried to keep my composure as I spoke.

I sat down then and stared at my hands for a few moments before I looked up at JFJ and told him, Jack would say, *"If you're going to do something, then do it right."*

I could feel Mark's hand on my shoulder and I reached for it for support. I held JFJ's gaze when I said, Jack would then say, *"Make it happen."'*

The young man with the eyes of an old man nodded. "You have my word."

Mr. Sanders gave me a big bear hug, then followed the Franklins out of the café. I remained in my chair, feeling numb, looking at Mark, Ellie, and Anna without knowing what to say.

Finally Mark spoke. "Jack would be so proud of you—as we are. Meg, this has been a long time coming. We all know that it took a whole lot of courage for that young man to face you and say what he was feeling. We all know he can't undo what he did, but I believe he will do well in this world now."

Mark admitted something that surprised me, despite the many years I had known him. "I've often thought about how Jack and I had a beer too many in college," he said. "Thankfully, we didn't always have a car to drive. Would we have been that stupid? I'd like to think we would have been responsible, but we never really know, do we? JFJ isn't an alcoholic and wasn't a repeat offender. He was a smart, stupid kid who drank to celebrate his college graduation day and then made a life-shattering mistake. He made something of himself while he was still in prison, and he seems willing to pay for his mistake in valuable ways."

CHAPTER 15

Saturday

Ellie arrived early this morning with coffees and apricot vanilla muffins still warm from the oven. I knew that she was checking on me. She and Mark had walked me home last night and stayed for a long talk about the ways to rebuild a life and the ways they believed I had begun the process. Afterwards, I barely slept. Pictures flashed through my head all night: scenes from my life with Jack, the image of JFJ's face and clenched hands, the tragic look on his father's face, and, lastly, views of my healing garden. But when the sun rose and promised a lovely day, I eased myself out of bed.

"Thank you, Ellie! I really need food—and nothing is better than your food," I told my best friend. We often laugh about all of the sweets we consume—but we tell ourselves that we walk it all off running between Marigold's, Annabelle's, and our homes. In between the everyday chitchat of the early morning, I was replaying everything from the evening before in my head. Once again we talked about JFJ's apology and plans, but after a few minutes, the kitchen suddenly seemed too confining. I jumped up and said to

Ellie, "It's a lovely day. Let's walk out to the garden and discuss our new friends and the writers' retreat.

She smiled as I grabbed my ever-present legal pad and pen. We took a quick survey of what was blooming and what new shoots and plants were appearing in the garden, and then we started on plans for the retreat, talking over each other, as we do when we're excited. "Yes," I thought to myself, "It's a new day with a new promise. We have a new topic now. Let's do our best."

Having never attended a writers' retreat, we wondered what that actually might mean in terms of time allocation, the space needed, the best foods for a spring retreat, and the accommodations inside my house. Those were about all the contributions we thought that we could help plan.

"You know, Meg, this is a new and potentially exciting revenue stream for our businesses," Ellie reminded me.

"I don't actually think we'll make that much," I said. "This is really more about hosting our new best friends. But it could lead to other retreats.

We decided to make a list of topics to have ready for our skype call the next day.

"A Writer's Retreat at our Bed and Breakfast, huh?" Ellie said thoughtfully.

"Well, I'm not ready to commit to that and a thriving interior design business," I said, laughing at the thoughtful look on my friend's face. When Ellie has a thought, it very soon becomes an action. "Right now I'm grateful that the retreat will only be a few days long. That way, I won't be changing sheets every day. Towels, yes, but I can handle the extra laundry.

"Why don't I send Anna over early each morning, to deliver a breakfast box?" Ellie suggested. "She can leave them on the kitchen table, ready when the writers get up."

"I'll make coffee and hot tea and have orange juice available," I continued her thought. "Then they can get to work early. They're welcome to enjoy the garden while writing, and if it rains, they can spread out throughout the house or move to the farm table in Marigold's."

For the lunch break and to stretch their legs, we assumed and they would walk over to Annabelle's. Ellie promised to create some new recipes to add to her already amazing assortment of sandwiches, soups, salads, and desserts.

Next, we discussed how the afternoon would go. Would they write until maybe three to four o'clock and then need a break?

"For the evenings, they could take the trolley to see the city, shop, and try a different restaurant every night. I could print out some menus from the internet so they could plan where to go and make a list of the sights and shops to see," I suggested, writing the ideas down under "To-Do List." "I wonder if they'll want to come back and write in the garden or just sit and talk."

"The only expense on our part involves the laundry detergent, beverages, and food," Ellie said. "Though you'll have the brunt of the work, doing the laundry with daily towels and the bed linens after they leave, and preparing beverages, followed by clean-up."

"I can handle that, maybe with a little help from Anna" I said. We agreed that we would hire Anna for laundry duty and breakfast delivery this first trial run.

"Okay," we laughed, "we have a whole new business plan we can develop!" We really did know that the accommodations in an historic old home and the chance to write, without interruption in a serene garden, plus the close access to Annabelle's, was an amazing opportunity for writers or other visitors.

"But, before we get carried away with our plans, let's see what their thoughts are," Ellie said. "By the way, what should we charge?"

"I don't know. Rooms at Ivy House Inn cost between $125 and $150 a night per person, depending on the season. So four days and three nights with breakfast could add up for four people." I thought for a moment. "It really isn't about the money this first time. Let's pay Anna and ourselves for the basics and ask them to make a nice donation to MADD. If we do this again, we'll have experience in knowing what to expect, and we'll establish rates.

"Is that okay?" I added. "What do you think?"

"Great idea," Ellie said. "But I'm warning you, we better start planning soon because I think this is an exciting new business opportunity for us."

Just then Ellie received a text from Anna, who said Miss Kate had called her, just wanting to say hello. "I invited her to lunch, Mom," she told Ellie. "I told her I'd pick her up after my morning classes. Expect us at one o'clock. Ask Meg if she wants to join us."

"What a hoot," I said. "These two will become especially close."

"Oh, they already are," Ellie said. "Miss Kate calls her Grand Girl and Anna will be over-the-moon-happy to drive her today in her yellow bug today."

"Let me give you a handful of blooms for Anna's little beaker in the car. Miss Kate probably hasn't been in a VW Bug, and will get a kick out of the beaker with a flower. Two soulful spirits have found each other." I smiled at Ellie.

"Yes, so very Anna, isn't it," Ellie grinned. "See you at one o'clock, I presume?"

"Wouldn't miss it."

STRONG IN ALL THE BROKEN PLACES
Ernest Hemingway

Part Three

THE
FIRST
WRITERS'
RETREAT

CHAPTER 16

Friday

The weather was perfect for the last week in April in Savannah. Weathermen had promised us that the skies would remain a clear robin's egg blue, and the temperatures were in the mid-seventies—warm, but not hot. Jenny, Ellie, and I had all been texting and skyping for the last few weeks as we planned the first of what we hoped would be many writers' retreats with friends. Ellie and I could hardly wait to see Jenny again and meet her three writing friends.

As soon as I opened Marigold's for the day, I began preparing for a house call appointment and a class later in the day—not to mention the start of our writers' retreat. Lucy was sunning herself. Coral roses overflowed from a vase on the counter. The cookie jar was full. I was ready for a busy Friday and weekend.

Ellie texted me again, and I could read her excitement behind the words, "Are they there yet?"

I returned her text: "Just as soon as they arrive, you'll know. Or come on over now, if you have café coverage" I knew she had full coverage, as we had thoroughly discussed this long weekend in great detail.

My appointment today was with Charlotte Watson, who had just moved into a new apartment— "small and empty," according to her. We met a couple weeks ago when she stopped in to browse through Marigold's. She said that a work friend had told her about my shop. We chatted as she glanced around. I asked if she was looking for anything special, which usually brings on endless conversation, but not that day. She seemed young and frightened, occasionally looking over her shoulder.

I offered her a bottle of green tea and brought the cookie jar over as I motioned to the farm table to sit and discuss her space and decorating ideas. We talked for a while, and then she asked me to make a home visit. Something was pulling at me to protect her in some way, even support her, but I couldn't quite figure out how, based on her demeanor.

I was still thinking about the mystery that seemed to surround Charlotte when I heard a car tooting the horn. Four women spilled from the car, and one of them was Karen. That was an unexpected treat. I ran out to greet them while dialing Ellie at the same time.

I shouted into the phone, "They're here!" Then I rushed to hug Jenny and Karen.

"I can't tell you how glad I am to see you again," I told Jenny, feeling as excited as a school girl. I turned to her mother. "Karen! What a surprise! I'm thrilled to see you, too."

"I know! I'm beyond happy to see you," Karen said, reaching out for both of my hands. "One of Jenny's friends couldn't come at the very last moment, so here I am, part of the foursome." She dropped my hands and reached over to hug me.

Jenny was talking excitedly, hugging me, and introducing her friends Kim Johnson and Lizzie Bingham, all at the same time.

"I'm so excited to see this retreat finally happen!" I said, laughing as I shook their hands. "So glad to meet you both. Ellie will be here any second."

And sure enough, Ellie dashed down the sidewalk at that moment, arriving in a whirlwind of excitement, laughter, and questions. The introductions and hugs started all over again. Jenny, Karen, Ellie, and I had become soulmates in a very short time.

I showed my four guests to their rooms. After they deposited their luggage and exclaimed over the antiques in each bedroom and the vintage jelly glasses filled with flowers from my garden on each night stand. Then we toured the rest of my home. We lingered in the garden just briefly, so I could point out prime writing spots, and then we walked to Marigold's. "It's a busy day for us all, and I know you want to get started writing without delay, but I want to just give you a sense of what we have planned for the long weekend," I told them.

The ladies exclaimed at some of the items in my shop, but I hurried them over to Annabelle's for an early lunch. They needed to stretch their legs after their flight, and the walk is lovely at any time of the year, but particularly in the spring. The ladies marveled at the old architecture and gardens, which were such a contrast to Indiana's in April. They spoke again and again about the warm weather and sunshine.

Ellie had set a table for six with her collection of mismatched, but color-coordinated rose dishes. All different pieces of vintage china, yet all with pink, red, coral or yellow roses. She had carefully planned the menu for us with new recipes and old favorites, and I knew our guests would love it.

The servers knew this was a special event, I could tell. They promptly poured sweet tea and then delivered a beautiful luncheon. Thick crab bisque was served in small individual soup tureens. Spinach salad with fresh strawberries, slivered almonds, and her special poppy seed dressing. Crusty bread with warm honey-butter. And, last but not least, Georgia peach cobbler. We took our time enjoying the sumptuous luncheon and catching up on each other's news. By the time we rose to leave, Kim and Lizzie both said at the same time, "I'm never going home."

"Oh, girls," Ellie said, modestly. "It's just soup and salad."

Jenny and Karen laughed and said to Kim and Lizzie, "We told you!"

Ellie remained at Annabelle's, so we thanked her one last time, and the five of us all headed back to my home. I wished them a wonderful writing retreat and excused myself to return to Marigold's.

I packed up my black leather Coach tote bag with notebooks, pens, colored pencils, a ring of paint chips, and a few handouts about decorating in a small space that I thought Charlotte might enjoy.

I found the apartment building easily, and I was thrilled to see an early 20th-century schoolhouse had been converted into apartments.

Charlotte answered her door and warmly welcomed me into her home. She was a cute girl, probably in her late twenties, dressed in a full-cut pink skirt and blouse. One glance around her apartment convinced me that she hadn't exaggerated. It was indeed empty. The unit, a small 689-square-foot charmer, consisted of a bedroom, bath and open space for a combination living room-dining room-kitchen. It was small in space, but oozing charm, with honey-colored hardwood floors, nine-foot-high windows with small panes, freshly painted old plaster walls, an exposed brick wall in the living room, and elaborate crown molding.

I commended her on the builder's choice of high-quality white kitchen cabinets with glass fronts on the upper cabinets, and black soapstone countertops with black appliances. Obviously these apartments had been designed with loving care. They oozed Old World charm, thanks to the exposed beams overhead and the exposed brick wall. Charlotte and I had our work cut out for us, however.

The only furniture she owned consisted of a very nice white slipcovered couch and a black wrought-iron double bed. A lamp stood on the floor next to the couch and a television was perched on a storage crate in the living room area.

Well, I thought, there is surely a story here.

I complimented Charlotte on her apartment. She invited me to sit down as she eyed my tote bag. I quickly put her at ease and pulled out my journal, pen, photographs, paint chips, and photo album. "Tell me," I invited, "what do you have in mind for your home?"

She startled me a little when her first words were, "Safety. What I like best about it is that I'm safe here."

"Yes, Charlotte, you are," I said. "I noticed the new security system in place to enter the building, and your heavy, old-fashioned door with three sets of locks. It also helps that you're on the second floor."

I knew Charlotte had a story behind her comment. I didn't need to know the whole story, but I did feel the need to help her. But we'd start with decorating. "Do you have a budget, an idea of what you'd like to see done first? Or are you open to different ideas?" I asked.

She took a few moments, seemingly to collect herself, before she answered. "I just moved here a few months ago after a really bad break-up. I'm lucky to be alive," she said bluntly. "We had only dated a few months. He seemed real nice. He had a very good job. But he quickly became obsessed with me. When I got tired of it, he broke into my apartment, one that I shared with a roommate in Atlanta. He destroyed everything in it. I had to get a restraining order to keep him away from me."

So, she explained, she moved back home to Savannah. "I'm starting all over again," she said. "I have a good teaching job here and I love my new apartment. I know he can't get to me because he is in jail, but I'm still scared most days. My mom and dad bought me this beautiful couch, television, bed, and all new white linens." She looked around the apartment with pride, I thought.

Then she added, "I love the cottage look, the feeling you have in your shop. That's what inspired me to ask for your help." She smiled for the first time before telling me shyly, "I have $500. Is that enough for you to help me?"

"Of course! I can't wait to get started," I replied. "We'll make this your cottage, a safe, beautiful sanctuary. And, most importantly, I hope that you can start to get some peace of mind. I think that we'll play off the black wrought iron and the black in the kitchen and accent with the color of your choice and white. How does that sound?" I asked.

She smiled, a new glow on her face and I knew thatI this would indeed be a special project. I considered telling her about the healing garden, but decided not today.

I asked her about her favorite colors, and she said, "I love aqua. Actually, this shade." She pointed to a paint chip on the ring of colors I brought. "It's such a happy color. Pretty and peaceful."

An hour later, I had outlined a plan for what we would call phase one, and she said she loved it. I told her about Linda's shower curtains and accessories and suggested that I would order four black and white pillows for her couch, as well as a black and white gingham shower curtain. I would ask Linda to trim them in aqua—"so they have a custom look." I also told her that I had a box of aqua blue canning jars. "You can use them on your countertops, to store rice, pasta, crackers, cookies, or whatever you want," I explained. "Simple but fun. They will not only serve as storage in your small kitchen, but they'll give you a punch of color."

I promised to look for a picture of colorful flowers (at least some of them aqua) that I could frame in a thick black frame to hang over the couch. "These are small, inexpensive items—actually, I'll give you the canning jars free of charge—yet they will give your apartment a homey feel right away," I explained. "With the bulk of your money, we'll find a small round table and two chairs for eating, a small end table for a nightstand, and a bookcase or open shelf unit for your living room, to hold the television and a few photos, a plant, books, or whatever interests you, Charlotte."

I told her about Anna's skills with a paint brush and suggested that we could ask her to paint a second-hand nightstand and shelving unit aqua. Charlotte said she liked the idea—"but won't they cost more than $500?" she asked anxiously.

"They'll be pieces that I find inexpensively at estate sales," I assured her, telling myself that I would stretch the $500 to the max.

"What about your time?" she asked. "I don't really know anything about decorating fees. How do you charge?"

"I'll let you if we run out of funds," I said evasively, knowing that this job would come out of my own "pay-it-forward fund." It takes more tha money to fix a feeling.

As I drove back to Marigold's, I couldn't help thinking about Charlotte. Scars, whether internal or external, tell tragic stories. I knew something about scars myself. I could hardly wait to start work on the plan for her urban cottage. I wanted to give her something to smile about.

As I walked onto Marigold's porch, I glanced into my garden and saw Jenny, Kim, and Lizzie with heads down writing in their journals. They seemed so peaceful. I noticed that Kim had a sprig of lavender tucked behind her ear. Karen was under the oak tree, sitting in an Adirondack chair while reading a book. She looked up, waved, and smiled, with a look of pure contentment. I could see the gold half-heart necklace against her pale blue cotton shirt, which made me glanced up into the oak tree that had caused such heartache. I thought briefly of Lovey and her half of the heart necklace.

Unlocking Marigold's door, I set my tote on the counter. As I glanced at the Friendship Board, I thought about Charlotte and the friends that she would make here in her old hometown. Yet again, I thought of the wealth of friends I had and how they accompanied me on every step of my life's journey. The best journeys, the ones that really matter, can only be undertaken with the help of friends.

By early evening, I had planned three more appointments, outlined my lecture for a new class focusing on antique accessories, and made a call to Linda to request the items that I had discussed with Charlotte. I was back in the storage area hauling out a box of canning jars for her, planning to wash them before the end of the day, when I heard Jenny call out to me, "Can you join us for dinner?"

"Of course," I called back. "Are you hungry now?"

"Starving," she and her friends said in unison.

"Then I'm at your command," I told them. "I'll lock Marigold's and freshen up a little. Then I'll be ready."

"Have you spoken with Ellie?" I asked as I made my way through the garden minutes later.

"Yes. She brought us the most delicious maple cupcakes while you were gone," Jenny said. "You'd have thought we hadn't eaten in a week, the way we devoured those. But, writing must build appetites, because we're all hungry."

"Of course Ellie found something delicious for you." I giggled, knowing that wasn't part of the plan, but what a lovely "greet treat" on the writers' first day.

We piled into Ellie's SUV as soon as she pulled up to the curb. "I know a great restaurant downtown in a converted warehouse full of atmosphere," she told our guests. "It's the best place in town for grilled fish served with peach salsa."

"Yum." I could hear the chorus of contented sighs.

CHAPTER 17

Saturday

As planned, Anna delivered the four breakfast boxes around eight o'clock in the morning. I peeked in to see cups of yogurt with fresh granola and berries, an egg scramble with cheese and chives in an insulated tray staying warm and cinnamon vanilla muffins. The smells were intoxicating and my mouth was watering. I already had coffee made, and juice and sweet tea in pitchers in the refrigerator staying ice cold. I had heard stirrings in the bedrooms over my head, but last night I'd informed my guests that I had to head to Marigold's early because I had a full day ahead of me. Besides, I wanted them to have their space, feel at home, and get their writing routine off to a good start.

On the path to Marigold's, I snipped two red roses, some yarrow, sprigs of azalea blooms, and some ivy to re-fill the vase in the shop. Lucy followed me into the shop, and I filled Lucy's dishes with food and fresh water. Sometimes she eats in the house and sometimes in the shop. I have a very smart cat. I think, since I often serve treats in the shop to classes and customers, she thinks that she has to have the same.

I took a moment to stand and admire my shop, realizing how happy and safe I feel here every day. Then, I took paper and pen and sat at the old farm table for a few minutes, thinking about my day. Charlotte was on my mind, but to my surprise, I also found myself thinking occasionally about DOC. I hadn't run into him since that one breakfast at Annabelle's. I had told him I wasn't ready for any kind of relationship with a man, so I wasn't sure why I was thinking about him. Maybe—just maybe—I would actually like to share a cup of coffee with him. It wouldn't be a date, not really, I challenged myself. Just coffee. But, I realized, another man had never entered my mind.

Until DOC, that is.

I decided that my first task of the morning would be to unpack the boxes of dishes that I bought at a fabulous estate sale the previous week. Unpacking boxes is always so much fun—in fact, it's at the top of my list of enjoyable things associated with my shop. I carefully removed tissue paper and newspaper, to reveal exquisite 19th-century French dessert plates with gold trim and pale pink roses painted on them. To my surprise, in the midst of the dishes, I found several small books of poems, some tea cups and a dozen tea towels smelling faintly of rosemary. Then, I found an small black satin evening purse.

"Odd, I don't remember these," I murmured to myself. "They must have been the last few items and someone just tossed them into the box to fill it up. I opened the sweet little purse and my mouth dropped open. Inside was a tube of ruby red lipstick, a stick of clove gum, a small key, and a wad of dollar bills secured with a rubber band. "Good heavens!" I murmured.

I counted the money. Eight hundred and fifty eight dollars! This must be some kind of mistake. I thought back quickly to the house where I bought the dishes in these boxes. I was reasonably sure I knew which house of the four had sold me these boxes that day. I was trying to consider what to do next when Karen walked in.

"You're not going to believe what I found amongst old dishes," I told her, recounting my story and showing her the loot.

Karen smiled. "This place—and you—just never fail to amaze me. Jenny and her friends are writing stories. You appear to be living stories worth writing about."

"Well, I guess you're right," I said, returning her smile. "This is a first for me, however, and I have rooted through lots of dusty old boxes."

"What are you going to do about it?" she inquired.

"I'm not sure. This is an odd-looking key, though it reminds me of something. Not a door key. Not a jewelry box key. Or a diary key. But maybe it opens a safety deposit box. I'll ask Mark— he's Ellie's husband—what he thinks. He's a bank vice president here, so maybe he will have an idea." I said. "Actually, I have a couple of appointments later today, so I may drive past the house where the yard sale was held and see if I can find any information about the owner's family. I think I recall hearing that the owner had died. It was a small yard sale, but it had some lovely things." I showed Karen the exquisite china.

"What are your plans today, Karen?"

"I'm spending my time thinking about another avenue of my career—or should I say retirement career now? So, I'm planning on getting on my computer and doing some research. I also brought a stack of good books to enjoy. And soon, I want to call Miss Kate and arrange a visit," she listed. Then she smiled. "But, in truth, mostly I want to relax and enjoy your garden and the sights, sounds, and smells of Savannah in the springtime.

"Of course," she added, her eyes twinkling, "I could go on a road trip with you."

"Yes," I grinned, "I think that's an excellent option." I suggested that Karen relax in the garden while I went to my appointments, and then I'd swing back to the shop for her. "We'll head in the other direction on our adventure, and see what we can find out about the little black satin evening purse and its mysterious contents!"

Two hours later, I found Karen waiting for me, rocking on Marigold's porch. I drove twenty-five minutes away, to an old neighborhood across town where I purchased the boxes of dishes. When I pulled up to a neat brick bungalow in an established neighborhood, I realized the house looked empty and even forlorn. The grass was higher and the flower beds weren't as immaculate as I had noticed them on the day of the sale. I distinctly remembered the roses surrounding the front porch, where a porch swing swayed and an American flag blew in the light breeze.

On the day of the sale, boxes, tables, and small furniture pieces had covered the driveway, and larger pieces of furniture had been placed on the grass. But on this day the little house looked deserted. I parked at the curb. As Karen and I walked up the drive, an elderly lady who had been cutting flowers from the beds surrounding the house next door saw us and started walking over.

"Hello," she called out. "May I help you?"

"Well, perhaps," I answered. "Do you know who lives—or lived—here?"

"I might," she said, with twinkling eyes. "But do you mind telling me who you are first?"

I felt like a schoolgirl caught sneaking into a classroom late. "I'm sorry," I replied. "I'm Meghan Kingston. I was here for the yard sale recently, and I found something that I wanted to return to the owner or the owner's family."

"Stella Jefferson lived here for more than fifty years. She passed away early in February," the woman replied. "Her daughter Mary Ann lives out of state, but she'll be here in a few days to finish cleaning out her mother's house and to meet with a realtor to discuss putting the house on the market to sell."

I gazed up at the empty windows of Stella's house, thinking.

"May I ask what you found?" the neighbor asked. "Stella was my best friend, and we didn't have any secrets."

I slowly pulled the black satin purse out of my Coach bag. "I bought several boxes of gold-rimmed dessert dishes here, but in one box I found a few other items, including this lovely little black satin evening purse."

"I never saw Stella carry that," the neighbor said with interest. "She and I never lived the kind of lives that required evening purses."

"It contained some cash and a key that could be important," I said.

"Oh, my!" Her eyes opened wide. "To my knowledge, Stella never had much money. She was very, very frugal. But I heard her calling out to me as the emergency medical people put her in the ambulance. She kept saying something about her purse over and over again."

The woman shook her head. "I thought she meant the purse that she always carried, a black leather shoulder bag, I assumed she wanted it because it contained her wallet and insurance cards. But when I handed that purse to her, she kept shaking her head, repeating, 'My purse! My purse! The black one.'"

"Had she been ill?" Karen asked, sympathy in her voice.

"No, she seemed perfectly healthy until that morning. Sadly, she died before she arrived at the hospital, they told me that she had a stroke. I quickly called Mary Ann." The neighbor wiped her eyes on a handkerchief she fished out of her pocket. "Mary Ann flew here immediately from New York." she said.

"I'm wondering if this might have been the purse that she wanted someone to know about."

The neighbor nodded. "Well, like I said, Mary Ann came immediately and stayed a couple weeks to organize things after her mother's funeral. She sorted what she wanted to sell and what she wanted to give away. This is a small house, but held lots of memories and lots of furnishings."

Her voice trailed away for a moment before she brightened and added, "As I said, Mary Ann will be back in a couple days to retrieve the things she wants to keep and to make arrangements to sell this childhood home of hers. You could meet with her then."

"May I have her phone number?" I asked, promising to call her and tell her about the purse. "I'll make arrangements to give it to her. She may have been looking for the key. It's a small one, not a house key, but perhaps to a safety deposit box."

"I know she'll be glad to hear from you," the neighbor said, returning to her garden.

Karen and I left the bungalow and drove back to Marigold's.

"What are you thinking?" Karen asked me.

"I'm thinking about what to say to Mary Ann. I'm not sure that we've heard the end of the mystery, but I think we will find out soon. As soon as I get to my shop, I'll try to call."

As we drove along, I told Karen all about the meeting with JFJ. She was as stunned as I had been at his appearance and the request, but I assured her that somehow I felt a new sense of peace after the meeting. Then we talked about the writers' retreat and the irony us meeting each other and Miss Kate, and how our lives were intertwined even before we met.

"Life has many twists and turns doesn't it?" I smiled as I thought that these new friendships were some of many benefits from those twists and turns.

"You're right," Karen sighed. "I never thought that my daughter would have breast cancer, suffer through chemo and surgery, become bone thin, and then, only months later, find new meaning, new friends, and a new passion in her life. I have loved watching her writing in your garden with such a happy, determined look on her face. Thank you again for this great gift you've offered us."

"You're certainly most welcome," I said, smiling at my friend.

"Just look at those budding authors," she said as we pulled up to the curb and walked towards the garden. "I think they're finding your lovely garden an inspirational place to write. I doubt they've looked up once from their labors. The aromas of your fragrant flowers must have a magical effect on creative people."

"I've always thought so," I told her with a smile as I unlocked my shop. I grabbed two bottles of cold green tea from the mini –refrigerator, walked over to the farm table, and began to dial the number given to me for Mary Ann.

"Hello," a pleasant voice answered.

"Hello," I replied back, introducing myself. "I live in Savannah, and I'm calling to tell you something interesting. It isn't an emergency, so I don't want to frighten you," I added quickly.

"Thank you so much," she said just as quickly.

"I recently was a buyer at your mother's yard sale. I'm calling because I found a small black satin evening purse in a box of dishes that I purchased. In the purse is a tube of ruby red lipstick, a stick of clove gum and a small key. I think, most importantly, a sum of cash amounting to eight hundred fifty-eight dollars."

"Oh, my gosh," the voice at the other end of the phone squealed. "I can't imagine what this is about. But I do know that Mrs. Niles, our next-door neighbor and Mom's best friend, told me that Mom kept asking for her black purse before she died. Maybe this is the purse she wanted."

"I met Mrs. Niles today and I understand from her that you're coming to Savannah soon. May I meet you, to give you the purse back?"

"Yes, of course! Thank you so very much! This purse must have had special meaning for my mother—I don't ever recall seeing a black evening purse. And I guess I need to find out what the key is connected to. However, the money is yours, as a reward." When I protested, she insisted, "That's only fair."

"I believe I should return it all to you—but we can talk about that when we meet," I replied. "When are you coming to Savannah?"

"Tuesday morning. I'm meeting with a realtor as soon as I get off the plane, and later in the week I have a mover packing up a few items to deliver to my home in New York. Could I possibly stop by your business on my way from the realtor's office to Mom's house?" she asked.

I gave her my address and tucked the purse into a drawer for safe keeping.

"You've certainly done your good deed for the day, my dear," Karen said. She then wandered out to her reading chair and her abandoned book. I greeted a few customers during the rest of the afternoon, spending the time between visits working on decorating plans for several new customers.

Before I knew it, the afternoon was gone. I looked up at the clock, surprised, when I finished scrubbing, rinsing, and drying the last of the antique Ball canning jars, destined for Charlotte's kitchen. I was thinking longingly about dinner. I planned to warm up some pasta and stay in for the night, but Jenny and her friends had other ideas.

"I've already talked to Ellie," Jenny said, closing her laptop when she saw me walking through the garden. "Mom and I want to treat you both to dinner tonight. "

"That isn't necessary," I protested. "This is a retreat for you and your friends."

"Yes, but tonight is for all of us. Then, after a fabulous Southern meal, we'll come back and sit out here on what will undoubtedly be a lovely, warm evening and take turns reading our manuscripts to each other, by the light of your tiny white garden lights. You and Ellie are invited to listen, if you'd like."

"I would be honored," I replied. "What time do you want to go to dinner? I need to shower and change clothes. I've been working with some dusty old glassware," I said, surveying the dust on my shirt.

"Let's plan to all meet at seven o'clock."

"Thank you again! I'll text Ellie and tell her to walk over."

We had a lovely evening featuring outstanding native foods. Ellie and I quickly added Kim and Lizzie to our circle of great friends. We listened intently as they described their writing. Jenny was working on a short article and a comprehensive memoir about her experience with breast cancer and her treatments and recovery. "I plan to submit it to a writing contest asking for inspirational pieces," she told us. Kim had outlined a list of questions she planned to use to interview nurses about their life experiences in the profession. "I've been a nurse for twenty-five years, and I plan to compile the answers from twenty-five respondents into an anthology," she said. Lizzie shared that she suffered from Multiple Sclerosis, and said her book would be a memoir about living for two decades with a chronic illness.

When the readings were completed, the six of us sat in silence, listening to the quiet sounds floating on the evening air. After a few minutes, I said, "All of you are such an inspiration to Ellie and to me. We are just thrilled to be part of your retreat. We, too, are making new plans for our lives and our own businesses—which we consider our calling."

I stood and smiled at my friends. "No creative night is complete without dessert! I have a simple treat for us, and we want to hear more stories."

We sat in the garden enjoying big bowls of lavender ice cream and quietly listening to Jenny, Kim, and Lizzie share their stories. Just as Kim's tale ended, we heard a car door close and saw Anna grinning from ear to ear. She ran up to hug Jenny and Karen, then turned to meet our newest friends. As I scooped another a bowl of ice cream, Anna kicked off her red canvas Toms revealing her purple painted toe-nails and sat on the ground, leaning against Ellie's chair. Looking around my garden, I couldn't have been more content.

CHAPTER 18

Sunday

Karen and I attended the early church service and then walked to Annabelle's. Anna had offered to chauffeur Miss Kate so we all could visit over brunch. Our Anna and the ninety-three-year-old Miss Kate had established a sweet relationship, which Ellie and I thought was adorable.

Karen and I arrived just after Anna and Miss Kate were seated in our favorite corner booth. Ellie joined us, and the five of us settled in with constant conversation. We told Miss Kate about Jenny and her friends writing in my garden during their writers' retreat. "Jenny is sorry to miss you, but she had something she was working on and said if she broke her train of thought, she might never find it again," Karen explained. "So she stayed with her friends this morning, but she promises a visit tomorrow."

Then Anna spoke up. "Miss Kate would like to plant some daisies in your garden after brunch, Meg, if that's okay with you."

"Of course it's okay!" I turned to Miss Kate. 'That way, you can see Jenny today and meet her friends, too."

"You are all like family to me now," Miss Kate said, smiling at us all. "I cannot begin to tell you how much all of this means to me. And Anna is a gift. She keeps me laughing with that cute yellow car. At my age, laughter is a great luxury."

Both Ellie and I smiled, knowing full well just how Anna can impact a life. She never ceases to amaze us with her kindness and generosity.

We all ordered something different for brunch, and talked about the special garden. Miss Kate looked around the cafe and commented on the walls, which were covered with famous—and not-so-famous—sayings that Anna had painted with a lovely swirling script.

Anna hopped up and toured the café, reading her favorites:

Raisin cookies that look like chocolate chips are the reason that I have trust issues.
Dance in the rain.
Color outside the lines.
Expect little and give more.

She was grinning ear to ear now, and so was Miss Kate.

"Did you paint all of these sayings, Anna?" Karen and Miss Kate asked at the same time.

"Yes, I did," she said.

"The customers seem to get a kick out of the unusual reading material," I added.

"I see my favorite," Karen said, smiling and pointing and reading, *There are the boys who stole my heart. They call me Mom.* "That reminds me of Jenny.

Her sons, Sam and Seth, are twenty-year-old twins who mean the world to her—and to me," she said, nodding to Miss Kate. I was sure they were both reminded of the sixty years of letters Karen had written Miss Kate.

"Those boys have been so good to their mother through the breast cancer ordeal and chemo," she said. "It was very hard for them to see their mother that sick."

But Karen had another favorite, she said. "The one by the door: *We all will miss you*. "That says it all, doesn't it?"

Karen then listed all the wonderful things here she would miss when the retreat was over: "Savannah. Meg's lovely home. Marigold's. The healing garden. Anabelle's wonderful breakfasts, lunches, and treats. The friends we have made here—you are priceless gifts."

Ellie and I smiled at each other.

"I just can't believe how this journey has unfolded. Who would believe it?" Karen said with love in her eyes as she looked around the table.

We finished our omelets, oatmeal, egg scrambles, French toast, fruit compotes, and assorted muffins, then sat back to relax and enjoy the last of the coffee and tea.

When Ellie rose and announced she had to return to work, Anna told Miss Kate, "If you're ready, let's drive around the block to Meg's."

Karen and I followed them out the door and reached my garden shortly after the yellow VW parked in front of my home.

When they arrived, Jenny ran up to greet Miss Kate. She carefully took her hand and guided her over to the table, to introduce her to her writing friends.

I went straight to the my garden shed and found a small spade for digging holes for the daisies that Miss Kate had asked Anna to stop and purchase this morning. "Daisies make the world seem like a happy place," I announced, when I saw the plants. "Thank you, Miss Kate."

The elderly woman beamed.

"Do you have a special place where you'd like me to plant them?" I asked, knowing the answer.

Miss Kate pointed to the oak tree. "If it's fine with you," she said, looking at me intently.

"Of, course," I said walking in that direction. Karen followed, and I noticed she was clutching her half-heart necklace as she put her arm around Miss Kate. They watched me plant in silence.

Just as I was patting the dirt around the base of the newly planted flowers, I heard Miss Kate murmur, "This was my Patty's favorite flower."

I smiled to myself. Somehow I had known that. "How fitting it is to have those flowers in my garden, then," I told her.

"This is for you, Lovey," I whispered with my final pat.

"I remember that you had lots of daisies in this yard when you lived here, Miss Kate," Karen said. "Patty and I would pick them and then pull the petals off with, 'He loves me. He loves me not,' and we'd giggle."

"Oh, yes," she smiled. "That was the summer when she had a little girl crush on Johnny."

"You're right! I'd forgotten that," Karen said. She seemed to stare in the past for a moment before saying, "But he was such a pest. Always pulling her pigtails when we would see him at the library or ice cream store. I haven't thought of him in years. I wonder what ever happened to him."

"What's his name?" I asked, standing up and brushing dirt off the knees of my capris.

"John Franklin," Miss Kate said. "In fact, he still lives here. He married, of course, and I believe they had one son. Actually, Johnny is now Judge John Franklin." Her words were said innocently. She had no idea about the way that statement would impact me.

Anna and I locked eyes immediately. I really was breathless at this new information. Judge Franklin, John Franklin Jr's father, had been a childhood friend of Patty and Karen.

"Did I upset you?" Miss Kate asked, sensing our look of bewilderment.

"No, you couldn't have possibly known this. His son, John Franklin, Jr, was the drunk driver who killed Jack. My husband," I replied with a choking voice.

I saw tears start to run down Miss Kate's cheeks, and I went to her with open arms. "I had no idea," she said.

"Of course you didn't," I said soothingly. "It is just another connection. So many threads of our lives continue to weave us together. I've recently met with his son, at his request. He is now out of prison and trying to make amends."

"How very sad for everyone," Miss Kate said quietly.

I nodded. "It seems that he had everything going perfectly for him, and then a bad thing happened to a good person. His thoughtless actions robbed me of the love of my life."

Anna picked up the story. "Jack was a great man. He was working hard to lobby for legislation to get drunks off of the streets and prevent just what happened to him. It was and still is all just surreal." She put her arm around my shoulder and spoke with a calm and resolution that I surely didn't feel.

We all fell silent, just trying to take in this latest piece of the puzzle. Finally, I spoke up. "All of us, all of our blended history, is what has created a bond that is indescribable. It is full of love, understanding, and continued healing. I truly believe that we are who we are because of the pain we suffered in our past. And, I added, "I believe we were destined to become great friends and have our lives intertwine in the future."

Everyone in the circle of friends smiled. "Well, back to work, ladies," Jenny ordered with a grin. She walked with Kim and Lizzie back to their table to resume writing.

Karen and I hugged Miss Kate a little longer than necessary before Anna walked her to the bright yellow bug.

"We will see you soon," I told Miss Kate. "And I hope you know that you are always welcome to come sit in the garden and visit with us. Anna, Ellie, and I are available to drive you any time. We love you, Miss Kate." I gave her one last hug.

"You've all been a blessing to me," she said to us.

As soon as I waved goodbye, I took my cellphone into the kitchen to phone Ellie and tell her of Miss Kate's most recent revelation. "Just when I think that I can't be surprised, some new piece of information or connection surfaces," she said. "What a small, small world it is, Meg!"

"I know," I said. "And if Karen hadn't made that innocent comment about Johnny, we might never have known the connection to JFJ. It was painful. But I'm also glad to know."

"Now, I think both of us need to get back to work, if I remember your schedule correctly," Ellie said.

"That's right! I have a class coming this afternoon for one of my favorite topics: Small Spaces. It will be just what I need: to lose myself in meeting new customers and teaching a class."

I was deep in my plans for the program about Small Spaces as I set my farm table with snacks, bottled waters, paper, pens, and handouts, when the door opened and in walked Anna.

"Hi, honey," I said absentmindedly. And then I looked more closely. "Are you okay, Anna?"

"Yes, I'm fine, and Miss Kate is back in her room watching a movie." She moved restlessly through the shop and finally blurted out, "I was just wondering if you'd like to have pizza tonight."

Pizza was code for "I need to talk," a signal that Anna had established with me as a young girl.

I knew the time wasn't right for a discussion here, with customers arriving on my porch at any moment. "Of course! Pizza sounds great for tonight. I have class until four o'clock, but then I'm all yours."

"Perfect, I'll pick you up then." She grinned, fluttered her hand in a happy wave, and turned to leave.

Well, I thought, something was up. "I guess I'll know soon enough," I murmured as I turned to greet my guests. Anna hadn't seemed upset, so I hoped that the discussion didn't have anything to do with this morning. Many times I've worried that all the traumatic events of my life that have unfolded before her eyes might be too much for a young girl to cope with.

The customers, six in total, had arrived promptly at two o'clock, and we settled around the table to talk about small spaces. I showed them a variety of photographs in a PowerPoint presentation while they asked questions. A couple of them had new condos and first jobs, but being very savvy business women, they wanted to maximize their space to work and entertain at home. Two were older single women. Two were married empty nesters and trying to downsize—which, I told them, doesn't mean downgrading. All of them listened intently and asked questions as we discussed colors, lighting, and tricks that seemed to expand space and still make a beautiful home.

At precisely four o'clock, Anna arrived and stayed at the counter working on the Friendship Board until the class members left Marigold's.

"I'm ready to lock up," I said, "if you're ready. I'm really hungry and pizza sounds great."

Anna drove us down the street, aiming for our favorite pizza restaurant: "Pick a Pizza." We quickly claimed the booth where we always sat, and immediately ordered our favorite pan pizzas and diet cokes.

"I see you're not going to live dangerously and try one of my other specialties," Antonio said, winking at us. That was the line he repeated every time we visited.

"Not a chance," Anna said, grinning back at him.

As soon as our meal was served, I got down to business. "Okay, Anna, spill it," I ordered. "What's on your mind?"

She took a deep breath before speaking so fast that I could only heard two key words: GRANT and CAREER. Then she immediately launched into how much she loved Grant. Occasionally she looked up to see my reaction to the word "love." But she didn't take a breath and I didn't interrupt, I just listened as she spoke about her love of art, most specifically painting.

She surprised me by asking, "How did you know that Jack was the love of your life?"

"Oh my," I said, playing for a moment to think. "We knew each other through college. We actually became very good friends first, much like you and Grant did. And then early in our senior year, we gradually started to become much more important to each other."

I sipped my diet coke and thought back over the years. "There wasn't a specific moment that I realized I not only loved him, I also was in love with him. We took care of each other with kindness and respect. We talked about a future together, but we both agreed without discussing it that Jack had to finish law school first. We knew that we wanted the same things in life, and we were willing to wait for them until the time was right."

I could say so much, but I confined my words to what she was hoping to hear. "Most importantly," I said, "we had established an unbreakable bond as we made plans. Perhaps that is why these last ten years have been so hard without him. I'm living the future we had planned to live together. But we're not together. And we never had the chance to build a family together."

Anna looked troubled for a moment, but I didn't want to turn the focus of the conversation from her to me. "Does that help?" I asked.

"Yes," she said, breaking into a smile. "Grant and I feel the same way. We aren't talking about marriage until I graduate in two years, but we are making plans. Since he is three years older and he's already graduated and started a good job in marketing, he'll have some money saved by the time I finish my degree. But," she smiled sheepishly, "I may change my degree. At least in part."

That did surprise me. "I can't imagine you doing anything but your art," I gasped.

"Oh, I'll definitely stay in art," she assured me, reaching to grab my hand. "But after all that has happened recently and some long talks with Karen, I think I might want to major in art therapy and use art to help injured patients.

"What do you think?" she asked when I remained silent, lost in thought.

Antonio came to our table with a pitcher of diet Coke, which gave me a minute to think.

"First," I said when he left, "I'm glad, as your Other Mom, that you come to me with these conversations before surprising your parents."

"Second, your parents will be happy that you aren't telling them you want to get married.....yet."

"And third, we all love Grant. He is a great guy, and the two of you seem devoted to each other. But—" Anna looked anxiously when she heard that little word.

"—I want you to be sure this is what you want. And I want you to be sure that you understand what dating is all about. Enjoy being single, being a student, and being in a fun relationship. Finish your degree. Let Grant get his career well underway. And then, if it is meant to be, you'll have gone through the steps every young couple should experience. And you'll still be happy together."

I could tell Anna was contemplating my words as I answered her second question. "As for art therapy, you will be brilliant, a natural," I assured her. "Ever since you made my 'WELCOME' sign, I knew you had a knack for changing people's lives for the better. Somehow, at the tender age of ten, you knew that I needed that." I smiled at her.

"Not to mention bringing Lucy into my life." I squeezed her hand. "Anna, you have always been a healer. I know that your parents will be very proud of whatever you decide to do in life, but you are talking about especially important work."

Anna mentioned the influence Karen had on her ideas, and I agreed that was beneficial. "Karen chose a long career in health care as a nurse working with injured patients, so she is an excellent resource for you."

"I guess we shouldn't let our pizza get cold," Anna said, changing the topic. Then she giggled, "Do you remember the first time we had a pizza date?"

"Of course," I said instantly. "You wanted to get your ears pierced and needed me to ask your parents for you. I didn't then, and I won't now, as you very well know. That is your story to share with your parent—except that this time you have my approval." We both laughed.

As we got up to leave, I hugged her and said, "Always believe in your dreams, Anna—but I know you will and lace them with love."

"You know I will." She grinned that special Anna grin.

Much later, as I sat in the moonlight under the oak tree, I said to Jack, with a smile on my face, "The days of white ruffled ankle socks and barrettes are long over, Jack. Our little girl is growing up."

CHAPTER 19

Monday

I was working in Marigold's very early Monday morning when Ellie called and asked if I had time for breakfast. I told her that since it was technically my day off and I hadn't eaten yet, I would be delighted. A few minutes later. I walked over to Annabelle's thinking about my new customer, Charlotte and how her life had been dramatically changed by a dangerous man. And, speaking of men, when I arrived, I immediately saw Ellie talking to DOC.

"Hello," he said with a smile, standing up and approaching me. "I just left the ER after a very long night, and I decided to stop for breakfast, hoping that I'd see you. Ellie was kind enough to call you at my request—so don't be mad at her." He spoke all that in one breath, glancing between the two of us.

"Of course I'm not mad. Just surprised. But pleased," I said, shaking his hand. "It is always nice to see you."

"Really?" he asked, staring into my eyes.

"Really," I answered, surprised at how calm and right I felt.

We sat down at the table where he had been drinking coffee awaiting my arrival. A server took our order, and the Ellie excused herself—to go in hiding, I suspected.

"How are you?" DOC inquired.

"Good! Busy with Marigold's. Plus, I've been hosting a writers' retreat the last few days for four friends from Indianapolis," I said. I explained about meeting Karen and Jenny, who brought Kim and Lizzie on their return trip to Savannah. I told him about Miss Kate. But I decided to not mention Lovey, my dear little girl ghost, whom I probably should start calling Patty. I gave him a little more on the JFJ update, and mentioned that he planned to attend the monthly MADD meeting, which would gather at Annabelle's this evening. "I'm really not sure what to expect, but Mr. Sanders made the plea to me to help this young man try to make amends, and I think he's right about that."

DOC nodded and seemed considering what to say about all my news, so I asked, "What's new in your life?"

"Same and more of the same," he said, running his hand through his curly black hair. "More sick and injured people in emergency situations. But I love working in the ER, and I really would not want to switch to a private practice with office hours."

"Not even on holidays?" I asked.

He shrugged. "I guess we all walk to a different beat of medicine, and I've found mine."

DOC was quiet for a few long moments, playing with his coffee cup and looking as if it held some answers for him. I waited for him so speak. I could tell that he wanted to say more, but I certainly wasn't prepared for what he said.

"I'd love to get to know you better." He smiled tentatively. "But I don't know if that would interest you. I wonder if that might be because I work in the ER where your husband died. Would my suggestion be unacceptable to you?"

I took a deep breath before speaking. "DOC, I told you that I haven't dated once since Jack died. I'm not sure how I can. I guess that I still can't imagine life with someone else. But I do enjoy talking with you," I admitted quietly.

"We both have to eat, so maybe this is a start. Let's just happen to eat at the same table." He smiled broadly.

I started to make a comment, and stopped.

"Please," he said, "tell me what you wanted to say."

I thought for a moment, then agreed to do what he suggested, remembering what I'd told Anna about relationships. "Lately I've done what I never thought I would do: I started to think about including someone other than life-long friends in my life. Someone who might be a man. Someone who…might be you."

I saw DOC's smile broaden and his look of happiness made me stop speaking for a moment. "But, DOC," I cautioned. "This is all new to me. I still have some scars that haven't healed—although they seem to be much better than I thought a week or two ago."

Without missing a beat, DOC said, "If you have room in your heart to get to know me, then we can work out the other details. Meg, I really care about you. I can't explain why I felt an immediate connection to you when we first met. But if you don't think you can care about me, please tell me now. I'll totally understand, and I won't bother you again."

He reached across the table to lay his hand on mine. Quietly he asked, "Who holds your hand? Who picks you up when you fall? You deserve to have someone do that for you."

I sat without moving, not knowing where to look as a warm glow spread throughout my body. I couldn't even breathe when he said softly, "Meg, I'm fighting for you."

I looked at my gold wedding band. But I didn't slip my right hand out from under his. I could feel myself smiling shyly when I said, "Maybe we can get to know each other. Maybe we can meet for pizza some evening. "

"I'd like that," he replied quickly, "Is there something special about pizza? "

"Oh yes. It lies at the root of all important conversations," I said, laughing. "I'll tell you about it when we meet."

"When? Where? What about tonight?" he asked eagerly.

"Not tonight. But Friday." And I gave him directions to the pizza restaurant Anna and I had visited the previous day. How ironic, I thought, that Anna and I had spoken of love in the past and love in the future—and I thought the focus was all on Anna. Until this moment.

"Well, Marigold's is calling, and you look like you could use a good night's sleep," I said, smiling into the eyes of the first man I had warmed to in fifteen years. "And, DOC, thank you for making Ellie call me for the breakfast. I could see my best friend staring at us from the back of the café, but I just waved goodbye. DOC and I parted at the door of his sports car. I turned down his offer of a ride. I needed moments to think about what had been said. And try not to feel guilty.

I found many ways to fill my day and postpone more thinking. Between customer visits, plans for new classes, and design assignments, I took quick little breaks to talk to Jenny, Kim, and Lizzie in the garden. This was their last day, and they were trying to accomplish as much as they could. "We hate to leave tomorrow," they all told me, together with a broad smile. Ellie and I made plans to meet them after the MADD meeting. We would listen to their last readings, which would be a capstone to the retreat.

By six o'clock I was showered and dressed in a green linen dress with a lightweight cotton sweater. As I headed back to Annabelle's for the meeting, my brain whirled with thoughts about the new friends in my garden, the man who insisted on invading my thoughts, and JFJ. I recalled all the heartbroken people that Ellie and I had met over the last ten years through MADD. She so graciously provided the space for us all to share our pain, plans, and goals for educating the public. I knew that most of the tables and chairs in the café would be filled on this night. I had established a fund from the many donations that started at Jack's funeral and continued through the last ten years, so family members who needed professional counseling were provided with scholarships to pay for these services. It was important to me to support this cause in Jack's name.

When I entered Annabelle's, I was greeted with hellos and hugs. I noticed JFJ over on the far side of the café, standing awkwardly by himself. I walked over and greeted him. "Please just have a seat," I invited. "We'll start our meeting soon. We always have a little business to discuss and announcements, and then I'll introduce you as our guest speaker."

"Thank you for allowing me to come," he said, his voice hoarse. He gripped his hands together tightly.

I nodded and returned to the group. After the president called the meeting to order and introductions were made, business and fundraisers were discussed, and newcomers welcomed, the president turned to me and nodded. When I stood up, I could feel my legs shaking. At that moment, to my surprise, DOC slipped through the door and took the nearest seat. He winked at me. I felt as if I could walk straighter and speak more firmly.

I felt Ellie take my hand and squeeze it for a moment. Then I cleared my throat and began. Gradually, my voice grew stronger as I spoke.

"Most of you know my story, but tonight you will hear the new beginning to my story. I would like to introduce John Franklin, Jr., who has requested to speak with us."

I scanned the room, noticing the faces turned in my direction and the warm, encouraging smile from the doctor in scrubs sitting near the door. I took a deep breath and continued, "I met Mr. Franklin informally ten years ago, when he was arrested for driving drunk and killing my husband." I saw JFJ cringe at the word "kill," and I heard audible gasps from the group as their eyes moved from me to JFJ and back.

"Recently, Mr. Franklin was released from prison, and he immediately came to apologize to me. He's here to tell the rest of his story."

I nodded to JFJ and sat down. The audience he faced looked both shocked and angry.

"I'm sorry beyond any words imaginable to find myself here and to know why all of you are here," he began. "But I came tell you that not all drunk drivers are bad people. Some of us are people who made one stupid, brainless decision that will affect us for as long as we live. That isn't an excuse, just a statement."

I watched bereft women look at him in his pressed khaki pants, cotton golf shirt, and polished manners as JFJ went on to describe the heady day when he graduated from a prestigious college with honors. He had been accepted earlier that month to one of the best law schools in the country, and he was bursting with joy and pride, he told them.

"And then good times went out of control," he proceeded to say. "I celebrated for too long, with too many rounds of toasts, and I had too much to drink. I didn't realize that, though, until I climbed behind the wheel of my father's SUV that late afternoon."

His story continued. He told us how he ran a red light. When he got to that part, he looked my way and gestured to me. "At that moment, I ruined both of our lives," he said. "And I ruined—or at least badly damaged other lives—more than I can count."

His voice choked up when he confessed, "I would trade places if I could with Jack Kingston. I told that to myself every day of the ten years I spent behind bars. But I can't trade places."

JFJ described how he completed a law degree in prison. "I can never take the bar exam or enter a courtroom as an attorney, but I can dedicate myself to finishing Jack Kingston's work," he said. He went on to outline his plans for supporting MADD's programs and for legislating for stricter laws regulating the sale and abuse of alcohol and the penalties for drunk driving, not only in Georgia, but nationally.

He looked at the faces in our group and said what all of us must have been thinking. "There is nothing to prepare you for a real-life tragedy, for hearing that someone you love has died at the hands of a drunk driver. There's no way to prepare you for a shattered heart when something tragic like this happens to your family. All that I can do is make a new path for my life that serves all of you, your families, and our community." He took a deep breath. "I'm so very grateful that Meghan allowed me start the first day of my new life with all of you tonight."

I was too choked to speak. I glanced at DOC. He nodded at me gravely, supportively. Ellie thanked him and he immediately left Annabelle's, leaving behind a silent audience.

In time, one bereaved mother said, "He truly seems to be sorry. But is it enough?"

I found my voice and surprised myself by saying, "I was shocked—horrified, actually—when he came to me to apologize. As you know, that was much too little, much too late. But, I've come to realize that this is the very best thing he can do: to make a difference in so many ways in the future. I've come to know him, and I realize he is a good person who made one terrible mistake. He has paid for that with ten years in prison and a lifetime of regret. I, too, have paid dearly for that mistake."

I explained that I learned that he wasn't a habitual drinker. He had never been charged with a previous DUI. He wasn't an offensive bully. And then I had something to confess. "I don't know yet if I can ever forgive him, but I'm willing to try. Why? Because this might help me heal, and help others to do the same. None of us can undo what happened to our families and friends, but maybe we can finally move forward a little at a time if we understand the other side of the story. Some of you are still in the early stages of grief. Some of you are like me; we are many years into our journey. The common thread is that we all are trying to survive and find a reason to go on and a way to honor our dead or injured loved ones. We are moms, wives, sisters, friends."

We were just finishing our meeting when Anna arrived. I was surprised to see her, because she never attended these meetings. She was carrying a large wrapped package and wearing a broad smile.

"Hi, honey." I said, then asked, "What's that you have, tucked under your arm?"

"Well, I heard you and mom talking about the upcoming fundraiser for MADD, and I wanted to contribute a piece of art for the raffle," she said, handing me the package.

"Oh, Anna," Ellie and I chimed together at the same time.

"That is so lovely of you."

Other MADD members surrounded us at the table as she unwrapped the plain brown paper, carefully uncovering the canvas. We became speechless when we saw what emerged from the paper. The canvas was covered with a background of soft, luxuriant pastel watercolors swirled together—pink, yellows, aqua, lavender, greens, and blues. On top of the lush background, Anna had painted a message in elegant silver cursive: *How long does it take to forgive?*

I gasped. And looked towards DOC. His face said it all. This was beyond beautiful. I knew instantly that every single person in the room was as overwhelmed and speechless as I was.

Silently, some of us with tears in our eyes, we took turns hugging her. "Well, this will definitely be the most sought-after item to be auctioned," the president told Anna before leaving the café with most of the others.

If ever someone was a natural at art therapy, it was Anna.

Ellie walked me back to my home. We didn't have much to say until I told her what I was thinking. "I constantly marvel at Anna's innate ability to know the perfect thing to say or do. She touched every life there tonight. I can't believe how well she does everything."

"She makes me so proud," Ellie said, her voice thick with emotion. Then she lightened the mood. She squeezed my arm playfully and said, "And I can't believe that your new friend—who, you must admit, hasn't been talked about as much he should have—came by to support you in the midst of a very demanding shift."

I just blushed. I honestly didn't know what to say, so, in my habitual fashion, I decided to change the subject. "I can't wait to hear what Jenny, Kim, and Lizzie have written this week. Can you?" I finished lamely.

"I know what you're trying to do, and I'll let you for now," Ellie announced. "But as soon as the writers' retreat ends, you and I are going to have a deep, one-on-one conversation. No interruptions, no evasions. We have a lot to catch up on."

I laughed and blushed and Ellie put her arm around my shoulder as we sauntered down the sidewalk. She whispered in my ear, "I am so very, very happy for you." Abruptly, as the garden came into view, she dropped her arm and said in a businesslike voice, "I think the last few days went well, don't you? It was fun bringing a different breakfast each day and having them join me for lunch at the café. They were always so excited when they arrived. I did my best to eavesdrop on their discussions about their writing."

I waved to the four friends, and when I got close enough, I announced, "I have some snacks ready: different cheeses, crackers, grapes, pear slices, and chocolate-dipped apricots. I don't know about you, but I'm certainly hungry. Now that I think about it, I haven't had anything to eat since morning."

Kim and Lizzie joined me in the kitchen, to carry out assorted beverages, ice, glasses, and a trays of snacks out into the garden. "Ellie," I called over my shoulder, "will you please plug in the white lights?" I could tell that Ellie was anxious to fill Karen and Jenny in on the events at the MADD meeting, and I was grateful. I couldn't talk about JFJ anymore that night.

As I set out the food and drinks, Jenny said casually, "When we came back from dinner and our evening walk, this blue leather journal was laying on our table."

I looked at the book in her hand, puzzled. "It doesn't belong to one of you?"

"No."

"Was there a note?"

"No. Just the journal. But we did see a lady driving away when we were half a block away. I didn't think anything of it—we had so much to talk and think about. And I've come to realize over the last few days that customers sometimes quietly come to your garden, sit a few minutes, and leave. I knew that we had locked the house when we left and that Marigold's was locked, so I wasn't worried."

"What kind of car was she driving?" I asked.

"A new-looking dark maroon sedan of some sort. I'm sorry, I didn't really pay much attention, other than to think that she didn't seem to be out of place in this nice neighborhood," Jenny said.

I took the journal from her hands, when my hands were free. Somehow I knew that this was another part of the journey—a very special component. But I really wasn't prepared to read the neat script written by a heartbroken mother telling the story of her son. I must have looked startled when I exclaimed, "Oh!" My friends gathered around me as my eyes traveled across the pages.

The story began with the memory of a young mother holding a beautiful eight-pound baby boy with dark brown hair. With love and longing, she described the ways the little boy grew and developed. She spoke of funny grade school adventures, playing sports, excelling academically and socially in high school and college. She wrote of her pride when her son showed her the acceptance letter from law school and of her husband's pride when they sat together and listened to the boy's plans for a career in the law. "Just like his father, whom he admired and adored," the text said.

The mother's story ended with the tale of a mistake that changed everything for her precious boy, her husband, herself, strangers, friends, and the community. "Good people do make mistakes, but what happens next counts for something, too," she wrote.

When I read the final line, "The story continues…" I felt so full of emotion that I couldn't speak.

A last note had been written in the journal. I read it with shaking hands.

Dear Meghan,

Please don't look back because we aren't going that direction.

The note to me was signed,
With love and healing to you,
Deborah Franklin

I collapsed onto the nearest chair. I could feel my friends' eyes on me. Finally, I said, forcing myself to sound normal, "Please! Let's eat and read. Ellie and I are anxious to hear whatever you want to share. Then I have something to read to you." I held the journal close to my heart.

CHAPTER 20

Tuesday

I had barely slept. Ellie and I were very reluctant to see our friends leave early for the airport. Lots of hugs and promises to return soon had quickly dissolved all of us into tears. They all agreed that it truly had been a great writing retreat. But, we all knew that it was so much more. We didn't say goodbye, just see you again soon!

As they pulled away and headed to the airport I thought about the journal. I had read it over and over again the night before until I memorized the words and images of that wonderful little boy. So many images and thoughts flooded my mind. I recalled the astonished looks on the faces of friends when I read the journal aloud at the end of our time together. It was the pure, raw emotion of a mother pleading for forgiveness for her only son, her only child, who was trying to right a wrong the best way he knew how, with humility and sincerity.

There was also an underlying message that pulled at my heart as well. *Don't look back.* Could this also be a sign about looking forward? About DOC? Was it a message Jack shared, telling me to begin living my life again? Was it about forgiveness? What about letting go of tragedy and helping others to do so as well? All those questions swirled around my head.

I finally slid out of bed. As I crossed the bare hardwood floors, I glanced in the big cherry mirror out of habit. To my surprise and delight, Lovey was there, smiling and nodding her head. "Yes?" I asked her. *Yes.* The word seemed to slip through the silence around me.

I kept my eyes on her, for fear that I was imagining her presence, but, no. She truly was there in the mirror. My little spirit of sweetness and comfort. I finally glanced from her to the pictures of Jack and me. But for the first time, instead of feeling wistful, I thought how very lucky I was to have loved such a fine man, and to have been loved in return. Perhaps the old saying "Roots and Wings" had some meaning for me now. When my eyes returned to the mirror, Lovey was gone.

I showered and dressed in a pair of soft, well-loved jeans and a cream-colored cotton shirt with three-quarter sleeves. As my thoughts turned to my calendar, I remembered that Mary Ann, the daughter of Stella Jefferson, a woman who once owned a black evening purse, was coming by to claim her mother's treasure.

I was watching a Monarch butterfly dance among my flowers while I ate breakfast—yogurt with diced peaches and granola—when I heard a car stop nearby. A woman of about fifty, with a mop of curly light brown hair, was heading quickly towards

Marigold's. I opened the kitchen door and started in that direction, calling out a greeting.

"Oh, I'm so sorry," she said. "You aren't open yet?"

"No problem. I was just about to head out here to my shop when I saw you arrive. I'm Meg, by the way."

"I'm Mary Ann Jefferson. We spoke on the phone about the purse you found," she said. "I can't tell you how surprised I was—and how grateful that you offered to return it."

"No one was more surprised than I was when I opened it," I told her. "I sometimes find odds and ends thrown into a box, but never a purse with money, much less more than eight hundred dollars. I was so grateful I could track you down and return it to you. I'm only sorry your mother didn't have it at the end of her life, when she was so anxious."

As I hurried to unlock the shop, flip on the lights, and open the drawer by the cash register, I chatted.

"The home where you and your mother lived is adorable—and take it from me, I've seen a lot of lovely homes. I just happened to pass by your sale as I was driving home from an appointment. Little houses make me smile. They always seem happy and cozy and safe, somehow."

Mary Ann nodded. "I agree. I loved my childhood, which is why I became a child psychologist. Although I never knew my dad, my life was full of love in that little one-thousand-square-foot home. It has two bedrooms, just one bath a good-sized living room-dining room combination, and a kitchen that was always the hub of activity," she said. By the distant look in her eyes, I guessed she was remembering moments from her childhood. Then she cleared her throat and her voice quivered.

"Then Mom had a stroke and I was too far away to help her. I flew home immediately, but she was gone by the time my plane landed. I was told that Mom kept asking about her purse, but everyone thought that she meant the black one she always carried."

I reached into the drawer, pulled out the satin evening purse, and handed it to her. I saw her eyes widen in recognition.

"I remember this purse!" she said. "Now, I realize that maybe she was trying to tell Mrs. Niles about this purse. I should have thought to look for it—it was a something special to us both during my childhood."

She explained that she had stayed in her childhood home two weeks after her mother died, cleaning, sorting, organizing, and making plans for the future. "I gave her clothes, shoes, and linens to church, and I set aside items for a yard sale," Mary Ann explained. "I kept all of the furniture that I wanted to take back to New York with me. Then I held the sale with items I thought someone else might want. This trip is to finish the last chores and arrange for painting and cleaning before the house goes on the market."

She studied the purse with a sad smile on her face. "I must have overlooked this little purse somehow. It meant a lot to Mom and to me when I was a girl. I sure don't remember seeing it—or you—at the sale that day but it was busy and several of moms friends from Church helped so I must have missed you. " she said.

"Tell me about your mother," I invited, gesturing to the farm table.

"Mom was an elementary teacher all of her career," Mary Ann said, as we both sat down. "My father died just before I was born. He was a fireman killed on duty. Mom did a lot of tutoring to earn extra money. She always kept her earnings in this little purse. She called it our 'mad money.' Sometimes it just bought us an ice cream cone, other times a new doll, and eventually, as I got older, it funded my braces and a prom dress."

She opened the purse, held up the stick of gum, and sniffed. "Mom loved clove gum," she said, inhaling the scent. "She kept this little purse hidden. I had totally forgotten about it until you called. I haven't lived at home for years, but Mom kept tutoring until the end. She must have continued to keep that money in the purse."

"Any idea about the key?" I asked.

"Mom must have a safety deposit box at her bank. She never spoke to me about financial affairs— I think she didn't want to worry me when I was little and she kept that up even after I grew older," she said turning the key over and over in her hand. "I'll go over and see if this key fits into a box." As she stood up to leave, she held out her hand. "I can't thank you enough," she said. When I reached out to shake the offered hand, she slipped the roll of bills onto my palm.

"Oh, no! I couldn't accept anything. It's yours," I protested.

"I insist," she said. "And mother would have, too. You gave me something much more valuable than some bills." She clasped the little purse to her heart. "You gave me back some very happy memories."

"Really, I don't feel comfortable accepting this," I insisted.

"Then give it to someone who needs it more than you and I do," she insisted.

A vision of Charlotte's empty apartment popped into my head. "If that's what you want, I know just who will benefit," I said, shaking her hand again. "I know she'll be very grateful."

"Well, it is a pleasure to meet you," Mary Ann said, preparing to leave.

"I hope you find what the key opens." I held Marigold's door wide for her. "Are you in town a few more days?"

"Yes, I'm meeting with a realtor to list the house, and I've arranged to have a mover load up the furniture and move it to my apartment in New York. I'll stop and see you before I leave, and let you know what I find." She laughed. "But I'm not holding my breath."

These days I seemed overwhelmed with thoughts about the new people, new mysteries, and unexpected gifts in my life. As Mary Ann told me her mother's story, I thought of JFJ's mother and her journal and her pain.

Barely two hours later, Mary Ann's car squealed to a stop once again in front of Marigold's. She hurried out of the car with a stunned look on her face.

"Remember how I said I wasn't holding my breath in anticipation of anything?" she demanded to know as she approached the porch and I opened the door.

"Come on in and take your seat at the farm table," I invited. When I saw her flushed cheeks and heard her pant, I asked, "Are you okay?"

I hurried to the mini-fridge to get us both bottles of flavored water.

"I'm just in shock," she said, clutching her heart. "A good shock. Meg, I can't thank you enough for calling me. You could just as easily kept the purse without seeking to return it. I might never have learned about the safety deposit box. But instead, thanks to you, I found an amazing letter Mom wrote to me shortly before she died. And I found more than fifteen thousand dollars in cash, all of it gathered into tidy rolls, held in place with rubber bands," she said, her voice catching on a choked sob.

"I don't know what to say!" I exclaimed. "How wonderful for you!"

"I know." Mary Ann beamed. "The bank teller counted it all and gave me a cashier's check. But the letter is far more important. It recalls her love for my father, how his death affected her, how my birth was such a blessing, and how she adored me."

She explained that the letter mentioned that all of the money was earned from her tutoring. "It seems that whenever the evening purse got full, she took it to the bank and started collecting all over again. Mom wrote that she was so proud of my work."

Here Mary Ann hesitated, but continued her story. "Still, she asked me to think about my life alone in New York. She told me that everyone needs someone to call them sweetheart, and she wishes that for me."

"You never married?" I asked.

"No. I thought about it a couple times, I came very close once, but I just knew he wasn't the right man, so I focused on my career. By helping kids, I felt as if I was invested in many children's lives, and that was an important form of love."

She glanced my way. "Are you married?" she asked after a slight pause as she saw me twisting my ring.

"Well, I guess that I would say yes and no. My husband died ten years ago, and so technically I'm no longer married. But when you still love someone, miss him, and can't quite figure out how to move forward, it seems as if you're still married."

She nodded, understanding what I was trying to say. I couldn't help adding, however, "This is an interesting time for you to ask me that question. Just in the past several days, I've determined to move forward. I've decided that it's time to pick myself up and reinvent my life. And I agree with your mother. It is wonderful to have someone call you sweetheart and mean it. There is nothing better."

"Big shoes to fill?" Mary Ann said, somehow knowing, "Did you have children?"

"No, we were trying before Jack died. And...well," I found myself rambling. "I've always wondered what the past ten years would have been like if we had been lucky enough to have a child together."

I continued rambling when I explained, "Recently I've been thinking about the fact that I have now lived longer without Jack than I lived with him. That is a startling thought." I stammered, wondering why I was unloading all my secrets in front of a stranger. "Well, that train of thought won't get us far, will it?" I said briskly, unwilling to dwell in "what ifs" any longer.

"I've spent some time there myself," Mary Ann confessed. "Perhaps I should start to listen to my wise mother's advice before it's too late."

With those words, Mary Ann stood and hugged me. "Well, Meghan Kingston, you have done your good deed for the day—and week, and month. I cannot begin to thank you for leading me to a treasure chest. I need to run or I'll be late meeting the painter. I may call you about your interior design business, if I decide to keep the house, it is something to think about. And, at the very least, I'd love for you to come visit me and dig up several of my mother's beautiful rose bushes to add to your garden." She paused a moment to survey it.

"There are more than fifty rose bushes at home, in all colors and shades. Gardening was Mom's passion, too. You're welcome to any you would like." She smiled and put out her hand. "You and I might have more in common than I originally thought."

I hugged her. Another story for my Friendship Board. "Come see me any time—there will always be a seat at my farm table waiting for you and an ear willing to hear your stories," I told Mary Ann.

It was late afternoon when Ellie called. "Any interest in having dinner with me?" she asked. "Mark has a late finance meeting at the bank, and Anna is off with Grant. I thought we could walk over to Robert's and enjoy their fish and pasta specialty. It's yummy. They just opened their new patio for dining."

"I'd love to. And wait until I tell you about Stella!"

"Stella, who is Stella?" ahe asked.

"Exactly," I said. "Wait until you hear this story."

CHAPTER 21

Friday

It was a beautiful morning as Lucy and I walked across the garden to open Marigold's. I stopped to gather some pale pink roses and magnolia leaves for the vase on the counter. Lucy stretched and went to make her self comfy in the warm sun streaming through the window.

As I started my day, I was thinking of the Indy girls and already missing them when I saw Ellie walking up to the door.

"Good morning my friend," she called out handing me a box of sugar cookies to replenish the cookie jar.

"Many thanks," I said grinning at her and our ritual. "And, for the coffee and treat," as she handed me a tall vanilla coffee in an insulated cup with a cherry scone.

We sat at the farm table and chatted, mostly about already missing our new friends and already thinking about the next Writers Retreat in a few months. Then Ellie said, "Tell me all about Doc."

"Well," I stammered "he seems like a really nice caring guy. He works in the ER and was with Jack when he died which shocked me at first but I've come to find very special. I've enjoyed these random breakfast encounters, thanks to you," I grinned. "And, we are meeting for pizza tonight, you know this is a huge step for me." I said looking in her eyes.

"Yes, I do know but it is time Meg. If, ever there was anyone who could understand what you've been through it is an ER physician. I love that he goes by DOC and he really seems interested in you. Just go with it and have fun." Ellie finished a little breathlessly.

'Okay, I will." I smiled at her.

Just then we heard voices and as they came closer we realized it was Anna and Grant on the porch.

"Hey, you two, " I called out as they opened the door carrying in a gift wrapped box and a beautiful Peony plant.

"What is this about?" Ellie and I said at the same time looking at Anna and Grant who were just beamimg.

"This is from your Indiana friends and we are just the messengers." Anna said.

" The gift card attached to the Peony told Ellie and I that it is the State flower for Indiana and our new friends wanted to be sure it was included in my healing garden. I was just speechless and then stunned again when we opened the box addressed to both of us. We pulled back the tissue paper to reveal photos of Karen, Jenny, Kim and Lizzie at different times writing in the garden. Each one of them had written a personal note telling us how much they had enjoyed their first Writing Retreat. The next gift was an Indiana cookbook with a message that perhaps Ellie might like to add a "Hoosier" recipe to her menu. Also, they had written a message with the request that Anna paint in on the cafe wall. It was simple and poignant, *"Friendship Binds Generations Of Women Together."* We were thrilled and then we saw the final gift. Smiling up at us was the picture of Miss Kate at Annabelle's enjoying brunch and another of her planting her daisies in memory of Patty. In a fine shakey print Miss Kate had written me a note. *"To Meghan, OUR home for the past, present and future. Love, Miss Kate."* I was stunned as was Ellie. We agreed that she is the most amazing example of both strength and softness.

"Anna, obviously you have been assembling this package for us and I can't thank you enough. I had no idea that you were snapping these pictures on your phone." I said. "Our new friends have quickly become important members of our family.

"Well, Jenny asked me to take pictures and the they all wrote the notes. The Peony was a thought after they got home so she ordered it and I went to pick it up." she smiled.

We texted Jenny and asked if we could set up a skype with all of them sometime in the next couple days. We needed to see their faces to say thank you.

I started adding the photos and notes to my Friendship Board. Anna and Grant left for class and Ellie and I walked to the garden as I chose a perfect spot to plant the Peony. We sat down by the old oak tree after I finished planting the beautiful deep pink Peony.

"I can't even begin to imagine how we can top these last few weeks, we've experienced just about every emotion I think," I said shaking my head at my best friend.

" Let me know about that," she said smiling, " after you meet DOC for pizza tonight."

YOU ARE THE HERO OF YOUR OWN STORY

The Friendship Board

Love Where You Live

Slipcovers originated in the South, to protect furniture from dust coming in open windows before air conditioning.

Rooms have to have soul—and that comes from accessories, photos, plants, linens, fresh flowers, pottery, and the beautiful patina of old woods and fabrics.

Never use blue in a kitchen or dining room because it suppresses appetite.

Never use green in a bathroom because it makes you look ill.

In the dining room, a rug anchors the table.

Know the needs of your room.

Linens serve as the table foundation. Layer dishes and serving pieces on top, blending new and old for an updated vintage feel. And, don't forget something interesting in the center of the table for visual appeal.

Nightstands or bedside tables should stand taller than the mattress.

Kitchen counters are the presentation of the kitchen. Consider the various options for beautiful countertops. Keep them sparkling and clear of anything but a few eye-catching items.

Place coffee tables twelve inches from the couch. They should be nineteen inches tall

Red, yellow, and orange are warm colors. Blue and green are cool colors.

When considering the types of lights to buy for a room, ask whether their purpose is task, function, ambience or mood. Consider their basic function.

Build a room, starting with a few simple, outstanding and useful pieces of furniture. You can change accessories inexpensively and create an entire new feeling instantly. Use three or four colors in your chosen palette.

Foyers make a huge statement. Don't ignore them when considering paint colors, pictures on the walls, and accent pieces.

Integrate the "R's" into your home design: renovate, restore, repaint, remodel, reupholster, repurpose, and remodel.

Mirrors appear to expand the space in a room.

Don't line furniture around the walls of a room.

Blend wood tones for visual interest: oak, cherry, walnut, pine, mahogany, and teak.

Table runners should hang six to twelve inches from the end of a long dining table.

Mix styles of furniture, but blend them.

Plants soften a corner and fill in empty spaces.

New construction can still have the heart and soul of an older home.

Old houses should be named because they still have a beating heart.

Book Club Conversations:

1. Who is your favorite character?
2. Why is she/he important to you?
3. Are you a collector or decorator?
4. Do you garden?
5. Do you write in any form? Short stories, articles, flash fiction or nonfiction, poems or memoirs?
6. Have you experienced a loss like Meg has?
7. Do you and your friends go to a special, welcoming place, like Annabelle's?
8. How would you have dealt with JFJ if you were in Meg's situation?
9. Do you feel the love and support of your friends?
10. How does your circle of friends compare to Meg's?
11. What qualities make a true friend?
12. If you could attend a class at Marigold's, what topic would you like discussed?
13. Forgiveness: what does it mean to you?
14. Discuss how forgiving is not forgetting.

ABOUT THE AUTHOR

Penny Davis is a retired health care professional who discovered a love of writing and found her second career. Journey Girls is a work of fiction but about all of the things that she holds dear, family, friends, healing, writing, decorating, gardening and of course brunch at her favorite cafe.

Share your comments about Journey Girls at
pennyindy@comcast.net
www.pennydavisbooks.com